The Way We Forgive

by

R. F. Whong

The Way We Forgive

Disclaimer Notice:

This novel is a work of fiction. Under no circumstances will any blame or legal responsibility be held against the author for any damages, reparation, or monetary loss due to the information contained in this book directly or indirectly.

Copyright © 2022 by R. F. Whong

ISBN: 979-8-88904-001-9

Published by Vidasym Publishing
A Division of Vidasym, Inc.
5013 S. Louis Ave., #532
Sioux Falls, SD 57108

Table of Contents

Dedication

I dedicate this book, first and foremost, to my Savior, the Lord Jesus Christ.

Furthermore, I dedicate this book to my brothers and sisters in Christ who have supported us in our ministry over the years.

Last but not least, I dedicate this book to my deceased mother, the true heroine in this book and throughout my life.

Why I Wrote This Book

Originally, I planned to write *The Way We Forgive* as my memoir. My personal stories were so extraordinary that friends suggested I turned it into a novel. Thus, this book is written as fiction loosely based on real-life events.

This book is a paraquel to *Love Under Holy Skies*.

What is a paraquel? A paraquel is a story that takes place simultaneously with another story.

As I noted in *Love Under Holy Skies*, many of the scenes depicted in these two books took place in real life. The divergence lay in the visa to Hong Kong: while Lily didn't get it, I did, and I went to Hong Kong to marry my husband.

Thank you for being a part of my journey.

Discussion questions for book clubs

1. **Family and Betrayal**: How did the aunt's betrayal in Ruth's youth shape her relationships, outlook, and later struggles with trust? Do you think forgiveness in such a situation is possible—or even necessary—for healing?

2. **Faith and Identity:** Ruth's journey shows a constant weaving of faith, science, and career. How do you see the role of faith influencing her life decisions, from marriage to career shifts? Can faith and ambition coexist without conflict?

3. **Health and Responsibility**: The story highlights struggles with chronic diseases, genetic predisposition, and lifestyle. How do you interpret the tension between personal responsibility and circumstances beyond one's control?

4. **Cultural and Generational Clashes**: Ruth and her mother love each other but constantly fight over health habits and discipline. How do cultural values and generational perspectives deepen or complicate their conflict?

5. **Perseverance Through Trials:** From professional setbacks to medical dilemmas and family crises, Ruth repeatedly faces difficult choices. Which part of her journey resonated with you the most, and what does it reveal about perseverance, sacrifice, and hope?

Blurbs from Readers

Whong's fictionalized memoir is a great read. While it reads like fiction, there is no doubt that you are reading this woman's life story. Against the backdrop of her everyday dual work roles—a trained biochemist and a side-by-side laborer for Christ with her pastor husband—we see a faithful woman with a busy, productive life. She treats us to vignettes of her childhood in southern Taiwan, plus snippets of her journey from university in Taiwan to receiving her PhD in biochemistry from Ohio State University, to marrying her husband. We learn about Chinese customs and history. We meet her lovely mother. It's a compelling story. Yet the essence of the story is in that which can't be seen or measured. As the seeds of a painful betrayal when she was still a child matured into a crop of bitterness and anger, she turned hard. Come experience the rest of the story as she shares the transforming love of Jesus that created a new life of love and forgiveness.

(Carol J. Nelson writes Christian women's fiction. The first two books of her Chandler's Grove Series are: Audra, Dying For Life and Audra, Life Transformed.)

This novel does an amazing job of portraying flawed yet lovable characters. Naomi, especially, is a pure delight as a funny, stubborn, generous, and loving mother. Ken, Ruth's husband, is warm and supportive. Jonny, their son, is sweet and lovable. Ruth herself is super relatable. She is flawed but loves her mother and tries to care for her family in every way possible—sometimes to her own detriment. The plot and pacing are good, carrying the story forward to an emotional conclusion.
I highly recommend this book to any Christian woman. I found it to be an easy and enjoyable read. It was heartwarming with wonderful characters and conflicts.

(Regina Rodgers writes Christian women's fiction. Her debut book is: The Gamble on Love.)

Chapter One

Chicago's North Suburbs
January 2010

I leaned against the white quartz countertop and breathed in the pleasant aroma swirling around the kitchen. Nice. The chicken should be ready soon.

"Wow, what's that awesome smell?" Ken hugged me from behind and gave my ear a light peck.

I stood on my tiptoes to kiss him on the lips. "My dear hubby, are you talking about me?"

He chuckled. "You and whatever is in the oven."

I touched his clergy tab collar. "Are you ready to leave?"

"I need to unlock the church's main entrance before others show up."

As he walked out of the door, I pulled the rack out of the oven, wrapped the golden-brown bird with a piece of aluminum foil, then placed the package into a plastic bag.

Wendy, a woman in her late thirties, contracted the flu last week. She graduated from my seekers' class about three years ago. With some vegetables and potatoes added, the bird should free her from the burden of cooking for one or two days.

The clock struck eight. Was Jonny up yet?

I hurried to his room and eased the door open to a slit to peek. He sat in bed and held his cell phone horizontally, a headphone plugged into one ear.

Engrossed in a video game? "What're you doing?"

He dropped the phone, horror scrunching up his mouth.

I pointed a finger at him. "Didn't you promise me you wouldn't play video games before Sunday worship?"

"I–I—"

I stomped into the room and clutched my hands together to suppress the urge to wave them in the air. "No excuses. A promise is a promise. Why can't you keep your word? Can I trust you? You're almost ten, not a little boy anymore."

"But—"

"You're still arguing?" I towered over him.

As Jonny covered his face and sobbed, I winced.

Lord, help me. Why can't I control my temper?

I shut my eyes to calm my emotions. Yet an image of my mother and me leaving our small village in southern Taiwan popped up, and my stomach twisted at the betrayal.

Auntie Su-Hua, whom I'd loved and trusted since childhood, shouted again in my mind. "You two killed my brother. Get out. Now!"

I shook my head hard to brush aside the painful memories.

No, don't overreact. Jonny broke one of our house rules. That's all.

"Mommy, are you all right?" Jonny hugged me. "I'm sorry. I shouldn't have broken my promise."

I dropped onto his bedspread, rumpling up the skateboarder motif. "I'm sorry too. I shouldn't have yelled at you."

He scrambled onto his knees and wrapped his thin arms around me. "I love you."

Warmth crept into my heart. I ran my fingers through his short hair. "Now, tell me. What happens when you break a house rule?"

"I have to pay a penalty." He groaned and surrendered the phone. "I'll give up my right to play games this afternoon."

"Good." I tucked the phone into my robe pocket, then tugged at his pajama shirt. "You'd better get up. We're leaving for worship soon."

A half hour later, we strolled through the arched doorways

2

decorated with a stained glass cross and stepped into the church's foyer. Jonny waved at me. "See you after my Sunday school class."

"Okay. Love you." After blowing my son a kiss, I approached Wendy's husband and gave him the food box. "Something for your family. Is Wendy resting at home?"

"That she is." Frank hooked the plastic bag's handle on his arm. "She mentioned you baked a chicken for us. This must be it. You're always so thoughtful."

I grinned. "Hope you'll like it. Please put it in the church fridge downstairs, for now, to keep it from going bad."

Linda, a young woman who recently came to our worship, stood nearby. Once Frank left, she wiped her hands on her black slacks as a flush swept across her face. "Mrs. Huang, do you have a moment to talk to me?"

Was she embarrassed? Why? "Sure. Should we go to Pastor Ken's office?"

With a nod, she clutched her purse to her chest, her shoulders curling forward.

I led her down the hallway, brown carpet softening the clack of her kitten heels, then gestured to the two wooden chairs before Ken's desk. Somehow, my mind conjured up an image of what my new office would look like if I ever dared quit my job for the biotech start-up company I daydreamed about creating. Most biotech start-ups struggled for survival. Maybe I wouldn't even have simple chairs like these.

Why was I thinking of that now when someone needed me?

I refocused on the young woman. As we seated ourselves with the door shut, she ducked her head and let her slippery hair shield her face. I broke the silence. "Linda, is there something you want to tell me?"

"I–I—" She sucked in a deep breath. "I met my husband a year ago at a friend's house in San Francisco."

Her head still tucked down, she dug the toe of her dainty brown shoe into Ken's thin carpet. Then she huffed and swept the hair away from her face, braving eye contact. "The easy manner he had around others impressed me. My friend said he grew up in a good family. His parents were teachers. I fell in love with him that week. After he left, he called me every day. Last fall, he proposed, and we got married. That's why I came to Chicago."

The dark eyes searching mine shimmered. Then a tear slipped free, so I passed her a box of facial tissues, my stomach tightening.

"Thank you." Linda wiped her face and tucked her hair behind her ears. "In the beginning, everything went well. I thought myself a lucky woman to have married such a wonderful man." Then, covering her face with her hands, she sobbed so hard that she hiccupped.

I retrieved a water bottle from the mini fridge under Ken's desk. "Are you all right?"

"I'm okay." She took a sip and calmed a bit. "I found he's into pornography. So disgusting and degrading. When I refuse to have sex with him, he either forces himself on me or walks out, saying, 'Who do you think you are? You're nothing. I have so many girls dying to have me. You should be glad I still want you.'"

A chill ran up my back.

"Lately, he became..." Her cheeks flared crimson. "Well, um, he wanted to take nude photos of me and videotape our lovemaking. He said if he has them, then he doesn't need to go to the online porn sites anymore."

I raised my eyebrows. "Did you give in to his request?"

"I'm not that stupid." She coughed. "He threatened to divorce me. I don't know what to do. I'm new here and only made friends with a few people at church, but I can't talk to them about this. I'm so ashamed."

Lord, how can I help her? I rubbed my neck. An inspiration came to me. "Linda, are you a Christian?"

Her hair slipped forward as she shook her head.

"Why do you come to church?"

She lifted her chin. "I passed by this building one day and saw the sign, Agape Chinese Christian Church. I was lonely and thought I could meet other Chinese people here."

"Has anyone shared our Christian faith with you?"

"No." She scooted to the edge of her seat.

A burden for her soul fell on me. *Lord, I need wisdom from You.* I swallowed hard. "May I share my belief with you?"

At her nod, my shoulders loosened up. "God created us because of His love. He wants to connect with each of us, but our sin prevents us from knowing Him. He's holy and has to deal with sin. In His salvation plan, Jesus Christ died on the cross in our place to pay for our sins. If we repent and accept Jesus Christ into our hearts, we can connect with God and receive the Holy Spirit."

She remained silent.

I gave her arm a gentle pat. "Do you want me to pray for you?"

"Will prayers help me solve my problem?" She stared into my eyes. "All these are new to me. I need to think about it."

Lord, what to do next?

I peeked at my watch. Worship was about to start. "Pornography is a tough issue to deal with and often requires you and your husband to seek counseling. Do you mind if I discuss your problem with Pastor Ken? He has professional training and may be able to help more than me."

"I don't think my husband will agree to it." She twisted her fingers together. "Please don't tell anyone about our conversation today."

I pushed back my chair, went to Ken's bookcase, and pulled out a new Bible. "Here is a gift for you. Promise me one thing. When you have time, read the four Gospels, beginning with the Gospel of John."

I flipped to the New Testament and showed her the page number.

"You're very kind." She slid the Bible into her purse. "Sorry to have taken up so much of your time. I saw you check your watch. Worship is starting now. Let's go."

Chapter Two

Two Fridays Later

As I placed the milk carton back on the fridge's bottom shelf, our landline pierced the early morning silence, followed by my husband's baritone. "Hello? Joseph."

I drank my milk and waited for him to end the phone call. Linda's image popped into my mind. Odd. I hadn't seen her for two weeks. Perhaps she'd be in church this Sunday, though I doubted it.

It happened before. After people shared their secrets with me, they could become embarrassed to come to church, even though I promised confidentiality.

"Ruth." Ken leaned against the kitchen doorframe. He scratched his chin, a habit of his when something bothered him.

I grabbed the edge of the countertop. "What's the matter?"

His brows furrowed. "Joseph's wife had a massive stroke last night. She's in the ICU. I'll go see them soon. Is Jonny up? Can you take him to school before work?"

A knot formed in my stomach and made its way up to my throat. Why did I dread bad news about health issues?

Unsure of my emotions, I took a step forward. "Sure. I'm off today, anyway. I have a doctor's appointment. Dr. Stone wants to go over my recent blood test results with me."

"Ah, I forgot." Ken pulled me into his arms.

"Last year, I still had normal cholesterol levels. How did it get so high in such a short time?" I snuggled against his chest, yet the sense of helplessness refused to lift.

The answer laid bare before me—genetic predisposition. All my relatives on my father's side suffered from high cholesterol.

"I understand. You love food and enjoy cooking." He patted my back. "I still remember the day you met with the dietitian. You came home with such a desolate look as if it were the end of the world."

I scrunched my nose and repeated the dietitian's words, using a high-pitched scolding tone she hadn't used. "'Ruth, you must consider your meals more carefully. Ruth, you must try to lose weight. Ruth, when you cook at home, avoid meat and seafood high in cholesterol such as shrimp and squid. Oh, and one more thing.'" I punctuated her final admonishing with an upraised finger. "'Ruth, don't indulge in sweets since you're prediabetic.'"

As Ken's chuckle shook his chest, I played with the button on his shirt, secure in his embrace. "You often joke I start to think about what to eat for dinner right after I finish lunch."

When I tipped my head back to see him, his mouth had curved up into an almost grin. "You didn't appreciate the enormous binder the dietitian gave you, did you?"

"How dare you laugh at me!" I swatted at his shirt. "After I complained I should stop eating altogether, you pointed at the pictures of lettuce and snow pea pods in the binder and told me they didn't have cholesterol."

Why did I sometimes behave like a little girl in front of Ken? Maybe because he liked me that way and gave me positive reinforcement?

"Did I say that? How heartless. I'm sorry." He pressed his lips together tightly, his expression serious again. "At least you're well disciplined. You went to the supermarket to load up on veggies and have been on a strict diet ever since."

My heart swelled. During the past two months, I'd lost more than ten pounds and brought my body mass index into the standard range. "I hope my hard work helps."

Yet from my doctoral training as a biochemist and my research experience studying kidney disease in a pharmaceutical company, I knew only 20 percent of the cholesterol in my bloodstream came from food. My body made the rest.

"Let me know what she says." Ken released me and scooped the keys from the pottery dish Jonny made in first-grade crafts. "I'd better go. See you later."

I glanced at my watch. It was not even eight. So early. Ken took his pastoral responsibilities seriously.

After Ken left, I dropped Jonny off at school and drove to my appointment. My teeth clenched tight like my grip on the steering wheel while I fought off the frightful scenarios racing through my head.

Uncle Tao, Dad's younger brother, used to lead an enjoyable, productive life. One day, he noticed his left hand looked gray, but he ignored it for a few weeks. By the time he went to the emergency room, clots in a vessel had cut off blood flow to his extremities. He underwent the amputation of three fingers.

I wiggled my hand to check for any sign of discoloration. No, nothing yet. Yeah, what a silent killer. I felt perfectly fine, even though my total cholesterol went above three hundred and my LDL, triglycerides, and HDL were all out of the normal range.

As I stepped into the medical building, shook the snow from my boots, and shed my winter coat, a lump still lodged in my heart.

Hugging my coat to my chest, I chewed the inside of my cheek and sat in the doctor's office.

Why did diseases and death scare me so much? Every time I entered a healthcare facility, memories of Dad's funeral and Mom's tear-stained face flooded back to me.

"Ruth." Dr. Stone's voice interrupted my musing. She wheeled her chair from before her computer screen and leaned across the desk toward me. "It's good you've lost weight. Although all four parameters have improved, they're still not in the normal range. Do you want to start statins or try dieting for two more months? Do you exercise regularly? A combination of exercise and diet will help."

Obviously, I opted for no medication.

When I trudged into our living room, my face must have looked as gloomy as the snowstorm that hit our area yesterday.

Ken sprang from his favorite seat on the sofa below the window and drew me to sit in the winter sunlight beside him, his expression no happier than mine. "Bad news?"

"Not good, but at least I don't have to take statins for now." The leather cushions were still cold beneath my slacks. I tugged his arm over my shoulders and leaned into him to warm up as I told him the details.

He gave my shoulder a gentle squeeze. "What exercise do you have in mind?"

"I don't know yet. Don't worry." I forced a smile, attempting to brush aside my own emotions. "How is Nancy?"

He scratched his chin. "Still in a coma."

"What's the cause? Ischemic or hemorrhagic? Does she have high cholesterol like me?" I brought a palm to my chest, another useless endeavor to subdue my trepidation.

After sixteen years of marriage, Ken got used to the medical jargon I tossed around from time to time. He sucked in a deep breath. "Hemorrhagic stroke. Got some pretty serious bleeding. She has diabetes."

"Diabetes is another silent killer. Mom has it too. I haven't talked to her for a few days. I wonder how she's doing." I should call. I kneaded my eyebrows and peeked at my watch. Eleven thirty.

Fourteen-hour difference between Tokyo and Chicago. Mom got up around six. I had to wait until at least four.

Ken touched his glasses. "We're having dinner with my aunt's family tonight. I told her you don't have to work this afternoon. She wants us to arrive before four to make dumplings together."

I massaged my temples. I'd have to call Mom tomorrow.

Four hours later, I entered Auntie's house and loosened my hold on Jonny's hand. "For tonight's sleepover with Doug, remember to have good manners."

"Yes, Mommy." Jonny saluted me, then ran to the basement with his cousin.

After hanging up our coats, Ken and I strolled into the kitchen. I picked up the chives from the counter. "So green. Did you get these from Chinatown?" I asked in Cantonese.

"Yes." Emily, Auntie's daughter-in-law, placed the chives on the chopping board and ran a knife through them. "Every time I hear you speak Cantonese, I'm amazed. Didn't you live in Hong Kong for only three or four years? How did you learn to speak Cantonese so well?"

9

"Lots of practice, plus an excellent teacher." I winked at my husband.

The chives' pungent smell filled the kitchen.

Cousin Albert elbowed Ken with a smile tucked at the corners of his mouth. "Shame on you. After being married to Ruth for so long, you still can't speak Taiwanese. How do you communicate with your mother-in-law?"

"Ruth translates for me." Ken gave a sheepish grin. "Taiwanese is a difficult dialect to learn. Very distinct from Cantonese or Mandarin."

"Excuses, excuses." Albert made a face with a cross between a smile and a growl. "How different can it be?"

Ken adjusted his eyeglasses. "Just as Chinese is distinct from English."

"Albert, give Ken a break." Emily laughed. "Isn't it odd that we Chinese don't understand each other's speech? But we can when the words are jotted down."

My dear hubby scratched his forehead. "The fault of our first emperor, Qin Shihuang. He unified the written language. Unfortunately, he couldn't go to each home to force everyone to speak Mandarin."

"True." Auntie reached for the chopped chives and mixed them into the ground pork. "Why does your mom speak Taiwanese and Japanese but not Mandarin?"

I took over kneading the dough. "It has a unique historical background. Taiwan used to be Japan's colony. My mom was born during this colonial period and received a Japanese education."

"But you never learned to speak Japanese?" Auntie leaned over to get chopped bok choy and garlic from Albert and added them to the bowl.

I shook my head. "By the time I was born after the civil war, Kuomintang—the political party of the Nationalist Government—had retreated from Mainland China and ruled Taiwan. At home, my parents spoke to each other in Japanese and talked to me in Taiwanese."

"Must have been confusing." Emily scooted over to wash the chives from her hands. "Now I understand why your mom immigrated to Japan." She came back to stand by me. "How is your job? You told me you dream of starting your own company one day. Any progress on that front?"

My fingers slowed down in shaping the soft mass. "I'm still thinking and dreaming. My boss treats me well and counts on me to bring him results. I can't leave yet."

Auntie placed the well-blended dumpling filling on the pearl-white countertop. "Ken, are your parents well? The last time I called your mom, she said her arthritis improved after she learned the *Baduanjin* qigong exercise. Does she still practice it every day?"

Ken snagged a mini pineapple cake from the counter and plopped it into his mouth, winking at me when I rolled my eyes. Then he wiped his hands on a towel and swallowed before answering. "Yeah. She also urges us to do it."

As our chats turned to wellness, I relayed my earlier conversation with Dr. Stone.

"Try the ancient Chinese remedy." Auntie moved to my side and slipped her arm around me. "It works well for many of my friends."

She launched into detailed descriptions of her friends' conditions and the remedy's beneficial effect. "Very simple. Buy a juicer and drink a cup of juice made from one cucumber, one bitter melon, one green pepper, a bunch of celery, and an apple."

It sounded easy enough. Plus, the recipe seemed harmless even though the idea of the concoction's taste made me shudder.

"Excellent suggestion." Ken flashed a toothy grin. "Hey, your birthday is coming up soon. I'll buy you a juicer."

A juicer? Not a diamond ring or a Gucci bag? Well, when did he give me jewelry for my birthday or Christmas? And a Gucci bag? Never.

We were practical people. Flowers for Mother's Day? No, they wilted easily. Instead, one year Ken bought me a silver-inch plant. What a drought-resistant plant! We came home from a month-long vacation and found it not only alive but also in perfect health to engulf the entire patio.

I bit my lip and punched the dough with one quick strike.

***

The next afternoon, Nancy came out of her coma. When Ken asked me if I wanted to go with him to visit her, I brought with us a container of a silver-inch that I propagated from a cutting. Nancy was asleep with tubes attached to her body, her face as white as snow.

"Pastor Ken and Mrs. Huang, thank you for coming." Joseph put the pot on the windowsill. "Such a healthy plant. Thanks a lot."

Healthy seemed a thoughtless word to use in a place like this, but at least the plant offered some color to the sterile setting. I kept my steps light so my sneakers didn't squeak as I crossed the room. I grasped Nancy's icy hand. "Does she need more blankets?"

Joseph hurried to a chair and brought a throw to tuck around her. "The doctor said a stroke can affect her ability to regulate body temperature. The damage is on the right side of her brain. She'll have problems with movement and sensation on her left side."

"At least her speech and language skills won't be affected." I drew the information from my memory bank.

Joseph grimaced. "But she may never fully recover. They'll put her into a rehabilitation program soon. They suggested I find a nursing facility to help her after she's discharged." He raked his fingers through his thin graying hair, then let the arm fall idle to his side as if he didn't have the energy to hold it up. "As much as I want to bring her home. I don't know what to do."

"It's a tough decision." With an understanding nod, Ken patted Joseph's back. "Let's ask the Lord for His guidance."

We gathered around Nancy and prayed, pleading for God's protection over her and for Joseph to make the best arrangements for their family. But I couldn't help opening my eyes and peering at the woman on the bed, her frail image seeming to sear its place in my vision.

Still unable to rid Nancy from my mind on our way back, I brushed the shivers from my shoulders and cranked up the heat in our Toyota Highlander. "Joseph has a tough journey ahead of him. As a caregiver, he'll be the one to provide the support for Nancy's recovery and rehabilitation."

"Yeah. Won't be easy." Ken flicked on his turn signal, then merged onto Milwaukee Road, slush slopping beneath the tires. "Are you calling Mom soon?"

I checked my watch. Almost four thirty. "Sure. Once we get home."

As I stepped down from the entryway into our living room, our landline phone rang.

"Mimi." Mom spoke without greeting me when I picked up the receiver. Mimi had been my family's nickname for me for as long as I could remember. "We'll need to pray for your uncle Pei."

Uncle Pei, my father's youngest brother, was in his late sixties. Like my mom, he, his wife, and their daughter, Yuko, immigrated to Japan and lived in a town about twenty miles away from Tokyo.

My stomach tightening, I pressed the phone to my ear. "What's happened?"

"Yuko called me early this morning. Pei had a heart attack." Mom's sigh whooshed through the speaker. "She said it wasn't serious, but I'll go see him in the hospital, anyway."

"Please give them my regards. Hope he'll recover soon." I drew my eyebrows tight, then pressed cold fingers to the pinched skin. "How about you? How is your diabetes? Do you watch your diet and exercise daily?"

"I'm fine." Something like papers rustled during her pause. "I'm leaving for the train station in a few minutes. Let's talk later."

I swallowed hard. "When you have a moment, please call me again."

After she hung up, I slumped onto the sofa and rubbed the back of my neck, a useless attempt to suppress the apprehension inside of me.

Why did I feel on the edge of panic when I heard about a traumatic event?

Ken sat by me. "Are you all right?"

I leaned against his shoulder. "We've witnessed Nancy's ordeal. And now Uncle Pei is in the hospital. Why do we have to get sick and suffer?"

"You know the standard Christian answers." He gave my arm a gentle squeeze. "To avoid similar incidents, please start exercising today. I have high hopes that diet, exercise, and herbal remedies will pull down your cholesterol level."

I expelled a pent-up breath and went to the basement to work out.

Chapter Three

Early March 2010

On the morning of my birthday, I walked into the kitchen. True to my husband's promise, a brand-new juicer sat on the counter next to a bag of mixed vegetables and apples.

Yuck. Not even a cupcake—or a birthday muffin. Twisting my lips to one side, I followed the directions and whipped up some greenish gunk for my birthday breakfast. I'd just poured the contents from the juicer into a glass when my phone buzzed with an incoming text from an unknown number.

"Ruth, my husband has filed for a divorce. I'm going back to San Francisco. Just want to let you know I've been reading the Bible you gave me."

No signature. Yet it must be from Linda. As my mind skipped ahead to her uncertain future, I typed a reply. "I'll continue to pray for you. Please keep in touch."

I dropped my phone to face the unfriendly mixture. We stood there in a staring contest, that green stuff and I, before I got the guts to sip the bittersweet liquid. Ugh. I couldn't help but wince.

The landline sounded. Grateful for the distraction, I crossed the hardwood floor to answer, and my shoulders relaxed as Mom's voice sounded. "Mimi, happy birthday."

"Thanks, Mom." I took another healthy swallow of the concoction and shuddered. "What's up? How are you? How is Uncle Pei?"

"I'm fine. The hospital released Pei on the same day I visited him. He's better. The doctor warned him to take his cholesterol medication. I'm sure he won't forget anymore after this scare." Her sigh came through the line. "And I ran into somebody at the hospital. Guess whom?"

I pushed aside my cup. "Who?"

"Your aunt Su-Hua."

"Auntie Su-Hua?" I snapped and slammed the glass onto the table so hard it should have chipped. "Isn't she in Paris? What's she doing in Japan?"

Mom went quiet.

"Hello?" I dropped into a chair and gripped its armrest with my free hand.

"She married a Japanese guy in Paris." Her tone sounded thick. "She and her husband moved back to Tokyo earlier this year. We'll meet for lunch tomorrow."

Moisture blurred my vision. What was Auntie Su-Hua up to? Hadn't she caused enough trouble for us? "Why did you agree to have lunch with her?"

I twisted the phone cord around my fingers and held my breath, waiting.

"I've forgiven her." Gentle as the morning breeze, her voice shivered over me. "I thought you'd also forgiven her."

"Of course, I have." I stood to pace around the kitchen. "But forgiveness doesn't mean we can trust her or restore our relationship with her. She could do you more harm than good if you befriend her."

Mom huffed. I could imagine her kneading her brows. "It'll be okay. Plus, you always want me to share the gospel with others. I intend to share my faith with her."

Ouch. Worrying the inside of my cheek with my teeth, I lapsed into silence.

"Well, it's late here. I'd better hang up and get ready for bed." She yawned. "Oh, before I forget. I've booked my flight. I'll arrive in Chicago on the last day of April."

"Got it. Good night." I placed the handset into the receiver and swallowed the remaining liquid.

While the peculiar herbal flavor danced on my taste buds, I shut my eyes to suppress an irrational fear about possible unfortunate events that might jeopardize my or Mom's life.

An image of my childhood home with five bedrooms leaped into my mind. My toes curled up like my fingers. Yet memories rushed in, fighting against my body's protest.

Mei-Shan, Plum Blossom Mountain, a small village in South Taiwan, my hometown, a place I left behind so many years ago.

Dad's body in the coffin, Grandpa's sneer, the arguments...

"Happy birthday, dear." My husband's greeting interrupted my thoughts. "I'm glad you've begun to use the juicer."

"Thank you." I crossed my arms over my chest. "Thoughtful of you to remember your promise."

"What's the matter? Why do you look dispirited?" He smirked. "Was the juice so horrible?"

I moved to rinse the offending glass. "The taste isn't pleasant, but it doesn't matter. I'm worried about Mom. She's just called me."

He arched a brow. "Is she unwell?"

"She's well. She said Auntie Su-Hua is in Tokyo, and they'll have lunch together tomorrow." I rubbed my temple. The heaviness in my chest brought upon by my recollection of the past refused to lift.

"Oh, Ruthy." He pulled me into his bosom. "Let bygones be bygones."

I tried to let myself relax into his warmth. "I'm not hanging on to my grudges. I just can't trust Su-Hua. Mom may get hurt again."

"Mom is smart." He patted my back, his voice soothing against my hair. "In Taiwan, she's at a disadvantage because she doesn't speak Mandarin. It's different now that she's in Tokyo."

"You think so?" Listening to his even heartbeat calmed my frayed nerves.

"I'm sure Mom will be all right." He ran his fingers through my hair. "But I'm concerned that every time you think of Auntie Su-Hua, your emotions plunge into anger and bitterness."

Heat surged through me, and I pushed away from the haven of his arms. Every muscle going stiff, I jerked my chin up. "What do you mean? You never went through a similar experience. You won't understand."

Oops. What was that about? I ducked my head, unable to meet his eye. *Lord, please help me control my temper.*

Ken blew out a hasty breath. "Though we've been married for so long, I only know your dad died suddenly when you were sixteen. You never told me the details."

My shoulders stiffened, and a knot tightened in my stomach. "Such a painful time in my life. I never want to revisit it."

"But it still torments you." He stood still, his hands falling to the sides of his pajama pants. "I'm here for you. Tell me what happened."

Great. Now Ken's intense pastoral gaze bore into mine.

I tilted my head away from him and stared at my plants on the windowsill. Memories from long ago flooded me. Scene after scene flew across my mind like a fast-forward movie.

"My father worked as the chief manager in a bank, and my family was well-to-do." I sat in our breakfast nook and flattened my palms on the tablecloth.

He took the seat across from me, the chair legs grating on the hardwood floor.

"Grandma and Auntie Su-Hua, Dad's sister, lived with us. As the oldest son, Dad bore the responsibilities of taking care of other family members." My heart rate kicked up. Needing to do something, I grabbed a tress of hair and twisted it around one finger.

Ken raised his brows. "Why did they live with your parents, but not with your grandpa?"

"I once asked Mom about him, and she whispered to me my grandpa lived with another woman. She also said Su-Hua was a divorcée, a rarity in our village."

Still, my lips curled up as my mind turned toward those early days. "I loved Auntie Su-Hua. We spent hours playing card games in the evening, especially when both my parents got busy. Sometimes she went out with friends. With my mom's permission, I would go with her to explore the mountains, the lakes, and the tourist attractions near and far."

Whoosh! Snow fell from the pine tree limbs outside of the French door. The neighbor's dog started barking.

"I never suspected my dad, active and energetic, would get sick." A lump rose in my throat. My smile vanished, and I swallowed hard. "But during my first year in high school, he complained about persistent stomach discomfort. One night, I heard him and Mom talk at length about something in Japanese. After I queried Dad, he patted my head. 'Don't worry. Your mom and I met a superb doctor. I'll have surgery to fix my stomach problem soon.'"

Ken crossed his legs and laced his fingers in his lap. The wooden chair squeaked under his weight. "What happened next?"

Even after so many years, a chill crept up my spine. "The surgery didn't go as expected. Dad didn't eat well. Within weeks, he went from a man in his prime to a skeleton. He was on the brink of death."

Ken's large hand covered mine. "Didn't you say your father accepted Christ before his death?"

"Yes." I withdrew my hand from him to rub my arms, forcing goosebumps to subside. "As he grew weaker, he had nightmares about ghosts and deceased relatives. Grandma, who attended a local Christian church, asked her pastor to talk to him. He was baptized in bed. One week later, he passed away."

Ken scooted his chair closer and pulled me into his bosom again. I rested my head on his chest, letting my tears wet his shirt.

"Almost everyone from our village attended the funeral. The next morning, a quarrel broke out in the kitchen. I hurried over and heard Mom demanding to know why the house she and Dad built was not under their name."

I closed my eyes, hearing Su-Hua's icicle-fringed words in my head. "You two killed my brother. Get out."

My grandpa stood there smirking.

I sucked in a deep breath, a vain attempt to compose myself. "Mom packed a suitcase and dragged me out of the door. We moved fifty kilometers away from home to Chia-Yi and left everything behind, including family pictures and personal mementos." I squeezed my eyelids tight, but I couldn't push away the intruding images.

"Oh, Ruthy." Ken gave my back a light tap. "You went through a horrible ordeal with Mom. One day, you were the apple of your parents' eyes. The next, you became fatherless, kicked out of your home."

"I've loved Auntie Su-Hua since childhood. My mom treated her like a dear sister. And she betrayed us." I wiped my face with my palm. "Worse, we had no money. Mom found a dingy place for rent through a newspaper ad."

"Must have been tough to go from a large house to a tiny rental." Ken kissed my wet cheek. "Didn't your dad have a pension or some sort of savings?"

"My dad was a dutiful son. Most of his estate went to my grandpa." I shivered at the memory of the damp cement floor in the room that I shared with my mother for two years. "Mom and I slept in the same bed. Many nights, I sobbed to myself. I told her I planned to quit school and find a job. But she refused to listen, insisting my father wished for me to get a college degree. I had to live up to my dad's expectations and get into National Taiwan University."

"Did your uncles help?"

"No." I flattened my palms on the tablecloth again, pressing hard against the smooth linen as if it could ground me. "They probably knew nothing about our problems. Mom didn't allow me to bother them. She said we should grit our teeth rather than accept money from relatives."

Yet I hesitated to share more. For years, I developed an intense fear of losing my mother through disease and death. Whenever I woke up from nightmares, I placed a palm in front of her nose and mouth to feel the soft movement of the air as she breathed in and out.

"God looks after orphans and widows." Ken gave my arm a gentle squeeze. "You entered the best university in Taiwan."

"Upon my acceptance into National Taiwan University, Mom reconciled with my grandpa and aunt and moved back with them." Bile surged up my throat. "Auntie Su-Hua intended for me to go home before I left for college. I refused. She planned to parade me to her friends. I had no interest."

Ken reached for a Kleenex to dab my face. My shoulders relaxed, and I snuggled closer to him. His simple gesture brought a stirring warmth to my bosom better than any jewelry or Gucci bag.

My heavenly Father loves me, and my husband loves me.

Then Ken released his hold of me. "Have you seen Jonny this morning? Let's go check on him. School starts soon."

I sighed and followed him into our son's room. Jonny sat at his desk with his children's Bible.

Lord, thank You.

Chapter Four

One Month Later

Ken and I hurried into O'Hare's international terminal. The place buzzed with relatives and friends craning their necks to view passengers.

At the sight of Mom's familiar plump figure, I rushed over. "There she is."

She hugged me, then Ken. "Must be my unlucky day. I got stopped, and they searched my luggage. Of course, they found nothing suspicious."

Since she spoke in Taiwanese, I translated for Ken. When he smiled and asked about her flight, I translated for him. By now, they'd gotten used to the minor inconvenience of needing me as the translator.

Mom drew her brows together. "Long and weary. Sleep escaped me, and I watched many movies."

She looked worn out with dark circles under her eyes. A scientific article about how sleep deprivation increased blood sugar levels accosted me, and my chest tightened.

Hope she's okay.

"A nap will do you a lot of good." I hooked my arm with hers. "Let's go."

After settling into our Highlander's rear seat, Mom patted my shoulder and handed over a pink bag. "A gift from Su-Hua."

I rubbed at my chest to ward off the rush of disgust.

"Mimi, here you go." She dropped it on my lap.

I slid out a letter opener in the shape of a medieval sword. "So cute." Yet I couldn't help biting my lip.

"She bought it in Paris."

"That's kind of her." I tucked it into my purse and forced calmness into my voice. "How is she?"

"Not well. Tokyo is expensive. Since she and her husband came back, they rented a small apartment. They needed lots of stuff. I gave her a table and a set of cookware."

Huh. I crossed my arms over my chest, wrinkling up the almost-new wool jacket I bought from Goodwill last week. "You didn't have any extra furnishings in your unit. You bought new stuff for her, right?"

She flashed a timid grin. "The Lord has given me so many blessings. It's good that I can help others."

I hugged my chest tighter, heat rising to my face. "How did she end up in Paris? Why did she and her husband move back to Japan?"

"Remember the house your dad and I built? Your grandpa sold it and squandered the money on prostitutes. Following Grandma's death, Su-Hua didn't want to stay with Uncle Tao's family and used her savings to travel to France." Mom feathered shaky fingers through her newly permed and dyed jet-black hair. "I don't know why they returned to Japan."

Pivoting in my seat, I glared at her. "Are you sympathetic to Su-Hua?"

A sheen glossed her dark eyes. "I have sympathy for her. Like your grandma, she's a victim."

"But she said those terrible things after Dad's funeral—" The sound of the garage door rumbling open silenced me.

Ken helped carry the luggage to my mother's room. "I'll leave Mom with you. Yell if you need anything."

I waved him off, then touched Mom's arm. "Do you need to rest now?"

"I can't sleep yet." She stooped to unpack the suitcase beside her bed, sinking onto the beige carpet. "Is Jonny at school? I bought him a camel hair jacket. I hope it'll fit."

As she showed me a tan coat, I checked the price tag and frowned. "I told you not to buy clothes for him anymore. He's fussy about what he wears."

Ignoring me, she pulled out a navy sweater from the bag. "This is for Ken."

While my fingers brushed over the soft cashmere, unease tingled at the back of my neck. Mom always bought the best for us, even though she lived on a modest pension.

"You look unhappy. Don't worry. I've got gifts for you as well." With a teasing wink, she presented a blue silk dress, then stood and held it against her to display the full shimmery length.

"So expensive." I examined the tag and sucked in a deep breath. "Now we need to take a cruise so I can show it off."

"Will we go on a cruise again? Very nice. I've got the perfect ring and brooch for the occasion." She yanked a jewelry box from her purse to reveal two items.

The stone in the ring was a piece of colored glass she snapped up from an estate sale on her last visit. The jade? A gift I bought her years ago from San Francisco Chinatown. It didn't cost much. Still, my mother had given me a hard time back then. I could still hear her protesting: "Why did you buy this? At my age, I don't need this sort of thing."

I picked up the brooch. The jeweler had set the dark-green stone into a gorgeous gold frame. "I thought you didn't like the jade I gave you."

Mom slapped my arm. "Who said I didn't like it?"

I grabbed the ring. It weighed heavy in my hand, likely eighteen-karat gold.

She took it from me and slipped it on her middle finger. "What do you think?"

I couldn't help scowling. "Why did you spend good money to have two pieces of junk made into jewelry?"

"Who can tell they aren't worth much?" She continued to inspect the ring.

Resisting the childish urge to roll my eyes, I checked my watch. "I have a project meeting at work this afternoon. I'd better leave now."

"You didn't take today off?" Her shoulders slumped, and her lips wobbled before she raised her chin and shuffled to pull down the duvet from the bed. "No matter. I need to take a nap, anyway."

Back at work, I rushed into the conference room for my meeting. As soon as it ended, I hurried into my office and dialed Ken's number. "Is Mom napping?"

"Yeah, she's still asleep. Everything is well. Don't worry."

Wishing I didn't have to work today, I shifted my phone to the other hand. At least Brian allowed me to have a few hours off.

A wave of gratitude flooded me. *Lord, thank You for keeping Mom safe.*

"Ruth..." Ken paused.

"Yes, dear?"

"I know you and Mom love each other very much." My husband's tone sounded hesitant. "But sometimes it can be too close for comfort."

"What do you mean?" I tapped my desk.

"We know Mom is overweight and loves sweets. When she stayed with us before, you two fought over those issues almost every day. I hope it won't be as bad this year."

He had to be kidding me. I nearly slapped the desk. "She has diabetes." For crying out loud, did he need me to explain it? "From my research, she can better control her blood sugar levels if she loses a few pounds and exercises regularly. Insulin resistance may even go away with a combination of weight loss and exercise."

"True." The word drawled out long and low. "But did nagging help? Did she heed your advice?"

Though it was my turn to speak, I bit the inside of my cheek and held my tongue.

"We all want the best for her." Ken's voice seemed more gentle than usual. "Think about how to achieve that goal. You're analytical and sensible. My dear Ruthy, pray and ask God to give you wisdom. I'll also pray for you and Mom."

After he hung up, I threw the cell phone into my purse, planted my elbows on the desk, and pressed my hands to my head.

Who could understand the bond between my mother and me? Nobody, not even Ken.

I shut my eyes. Moisture built up behind my eyelids as painful memories invaded my mind.

For my college, I went alone to Taipei, the largest city in

Taiwan. During my first days at National Taiwan University, I rented a room from a young couple and got a job tutoring a high school student three nights a week.

One month later, Mom sent me a letter saying my grandpa and auntie Su-Hua wanted her to leave and she planned to move in with me. I checked with my landlords, and they agreed to let my mother stay with me.

Mom arrived, and I snapped at her, demanding to know why she let them kick her out again. When she said they got into a fight after she found out they'd thrown out all of our family photos and my diaries, I slammed my fist on the table and declared I'd never forgive them.

She whispered, "Your temper hasn't improved."

I didn't bother to respond and rushed out of our room into the kitchen.

Weeks later, she sat me down for a chat. "Mimi, you never go out with anyone. Your daily routine revolves around the library, your classes, job, and home."

What did she expect? No other college student lived with their mother in a rented room by the campus. My classmates saw me as beyond bizarre.

Her eyes glistened when I told her so. "I didn't think my staying with you would cause so much trouble."

"Oh, Mom." I grabbed her hand. "Don't say that. You're all I have in this world. I need you here. I don't care how others view me."

A knock derailed my train of thought. Masashi Suzuki, the Japanese research scientist in my group, peeked through my glass door.

After I waved him in, he approached, frowning. "Ruth, are you all right?"

I rubbed at a throbbing temple. "I'm fine." Yeah right. "Thank you."

"You leaned your head against the desk. I was concerned you got sick." He adjusted his eyeglasses. "I'm glad you're okay. I'm leaving for my carpool now. See you tomorrow."

I twisted my watch into view. Somehow, the heavier face always slipped to the back of my wrist. "Is it already five fifteen? I'd better go too."

A half hour later, I opened the door to our living room, and a pleasant aroma drifted into my nostrils.

Mom's slippers padded on the hardwood entryway as she came forward to greet me. "I've used the bag of shrimp in the freezer. Ken and Jonny both love my scampi."

I tossed my purse onto the loveseat nearby. "Are you cooking already? It's your first day here."

"No problem. The nap did its magic." She waggled her fingers, beckoning me to come see her dinner preparations. "A lot of snow pea pods in your fridge. I need to stir-fry them with pork, and dinner will be ready."

A knot formed in my stomach. I had to break the news. "I can't eat shrimp, meat, or anything greasy."

"Why?" Her eyes opened wide.

I forced calmness into my tone. "I have high cholesterol and must control my diet."

She placed a palm over her heart. "Oh, don't tell me you'll end up like your uncle Tao and uncle Pei."

"No. I'm determined to win the battle against this silent killer." I walked to the fridge to take out a head of lettuce. "That's why I'll have this tonight."

She followed me. "But you love food. You enjoy cooking."

While she started stir-fry for the others, I dropped the leafy greens on the counter. "To control your diabetes, you also need to exercise and..."

Ken leaned against the kitchen door and winked at me.

"Never mind." I bit my lip.

Jonny skipped into the room as Mom plated the food. "Wow, Nana's famous dish." He picked up a shrimp, ready to pop it into his mouth on his way to the table.

"Jonny, we have to say grace first." Ken chided him with a smile and took his regular chair. Mom's was the one to his right that sat empty, waiting for her all winter.

After dinner, Mom took the plates to the sink.

As she scraped out every crumb, I frowned. "We have a dishwasher."

"Washing by hand works better." She poured detergent into a bowl. Bubbles stuck to her bare hands, and specks of water splashed on her arms.

Huh. I squinted. Did I have to go over this with her again? "Most modern dishwashers outperform washing by hand and are more water efficient."

"Don't believe everything you read." She sloshed one of my Corning plates through the suds. "Machines can never replace humans."

"But—"

Ken tugged at my sleeve.

Right. I chuffed out a breath. How many times had Mom and I argued over this? With a nod at my husband, I took leave.

Chapter Five

One week later, after work, I placed the pill bottle on the kitchen countertop and flipped the package insert to the "Warnings and Precautions" section. As I expected, Lipitor's most serious side effect was myopathy, a dysfunction of the muscle fibers. I scowled at the troublesome sentences: "Advise patients to promptly report to their physician unexplained and/or persistent muscle pain, tenderness, or weakness. LIPITOR therapy should be discontinued if myopathy is diagnosed or suspected."

Dr. Stone's words echoed in my head. "Ruth, your cholesterol is still out of control. Have you been exercising?"

My workout routine included skipping rope three hundred times, weight lifting, and stretching, a total of thirty to forty minutes each day.

"I'm impressed." She let out a low whistle when I told her. Then she drew her brows together. "I don't think you have any choice other than to take medication."

"Mimi, what're you doing?"

At Mom's voice, I attempted to put the bottle into my pocket. "Nothing."

But she grabbed it from me. "So, exercise, diet, and the Chinese herbal remedy didn't help. The doctor has prescribed something for you."

I moved away from her to grab the juicer and pushed it to the back of the cabinet for storage.

Mom let out a hard breath. "Have you prayed about it?"

"I have." I grabbed a few green tea leaves from a tin can, dropped them into my cup, and poured hot water from our electric kettle. "Do you care for one?"

"No, thank you." She plopped into her chair. "Has God answered you?"

I stirred my tea, savoring the fresh grassy smell. "He did. The answer is no. He won't heal my condition. Just like your diabetes, we need to learn to live with it."

"I wonder how prayers work. You said God always responds to His children's pleas," she murmured, almost as if talking to herself.

"Yes, He does, although the responses may not be according to our wishes. God's reply may be yes or no. Often He wants us to wait." I reached for my Bible on the table to pull out a bookmark. "I made this. Sorry. It's in English."

Mom perused the words. "Tell me what it says."

I pointed to each letter. "ACTS is about the content of my prayers, adoration, confession, thanksgiving, and supplication. WEAR stands for willingness to obey, expectancy, assurance, and reflection—the attitudes I need to have when I pray. I think attitudes are even more important than content."

"Mimi, you've grown so much on your faith journey." Mom's fingers glided over mine. "Remember your college days? You struggled to find your way in this world."

"The years after Dad passed away will forever remain in my mind as the most difficult period of my life." I chugged a gulp of tea, thinking back to my childhood home.

Whenever a typhoon swept across Taiwan and the power went out, Mom lit a candle. Under the gentle swaying twinkle, Dad told me countless ghost stories.

I didn't doubt the existence of gods and spirits. The mystery was how they interacted with humans.

Yet after Dad's death, I didn't want God in my life. "I don't know whether I've mentioned this to you. When Dad got ill, I prayed to God, telling Him that if He healed Dad, I'd become a Christian."

"No, you didn't." Mom squinted.

"Dad didn't get better. I concluded God didn't exist, or He didn't care at all." My mouthful of tea lost its flavor. After that, I thought all the stuff about spiritual matters was pure imagination. I shut down and hid in a cocoon. "Remember, you used to drag me to the movies with you?"

"I was worried. You didn't have any friends." Mom scratched her head. "The theater close to where we lived ran old movies from different countries, with subtitles. I enjoyed watching *The Sound of Music*, *Gone with the Wind*, *Casablanca*, and many others. The movies didn't help, did they? I'm grateful that your friend Li invited you to church."

My lips crinkled up. Yeah, Li, a sophomore, was my mentor. In our first meeting, she treated me to a popular restaurant. I feasted on stir-fried shrimp. Following dinner, she asked me to go to her fellowship group with her. Although reluctance tightened my stomach, I couldn't muster up the courage to say no after enjoying a sumptuous meal.

Sitting up straighter, I sipped my tea, its sedgy flavor dancing on my taste buds. "I went to church with her and spent most of my time debating with people. I insisted God didn't exist. Even if He did, He didn't care about us."

Mom caressed the bookmark tassels. With her head tipped down like that, her freshly dyed-black hair shone under the lamplight above us. "You didn't want to believe. Then why did you keep going back?"

"Li, kind and persistent, didn't give up and continued to invite me." I placed a hand over my chest to calm my emotions. "After I'd attended church for six months, the fellowship group counselor cornered me. He had a good point when he asked if I was so confident I was right and all the Christians, including millions throughout history, were wrong."

I answered yes back then, but deep down, uncertainty seized me.

Mom tilted her face up. "Besides Li, didn't your professor, Dr. Lu, also have a great influence on you?"

"You remember her, even though you only met her once?"

"Why are you surprised?" Mom leaned forward. "I'll never forget her courage. She had cancer but devoted all her time to helping students."

Yes, Dr. Lillian Lu, my English professor at the university.

Every week I rode my old bike from our place to her apartment behind Grace Baptist Church. She was the church's music director and lived alone.

I vented my anger at God and life. She usually didn't say much, but listened with care and love in her eyes.

After I told her what happened to my dad and my fear of death, she patted my arm. "How old are you? Eighteen? You're still young, with a bright future ahead of you."

At the thought of my beloved teacher, a warm feeling flooded me. I sipped my tea again. "I don't think I've told you this before. A breakthrough in my faith journey came when I visited her one day. The chemotherapy had taken its toll, and all her hair had fallen out. Her once beautiful face lost its glow. I stared at her and realized in front of me sat a very sick person who might die any day. I blurted out, 'Aren't you afraid of death?'"

Mom put down the bookmark. "And what did she say?"

"She responded right away, her tone as serene as always. 'No, I'm not.' She said as a Christian, she believed in heaven, and her life would go on after the death of her body."

Moisture shimmered in my mom's eyes. "So wise and full of the Holy Spirit. Wasn't she the one who suggested you take Ruth as your baptized name?"

I dipped my chin. "My conversation with her on that day helped open my soul to accept Jesus as my Savior. I asked myself, 'How could a person at death's door be so full of grace? Maybe heaven is for real. Maybe what Christians believe is true.'" I hitched a deep breath. "But you didn't go to church with me. You hung on to your folk religion."

Mom picked up the pill bottle and spun it around. "Letting go of the influence from our background and culture wasn't easy."

"True." I drew a Kleenex to wipe my forehead. "Dr. Lu passed away shortly after I left Taiwan. I received the news in a red envelope from her friend. She wanted all of us to celebrate her passing because she believed that through death, she'd received the promised eternal inheritance from the Lord." I touched Mom's hand. "Li also lives in Japan. Have you seen her? How is she doing? I haven't written to her for a while."

"She and her family are well." Mom turned her fingers to squeeze mine. "I ran into her a while ago. Her two daughters are so sweet."

"Hi, Mom. Hi, Ruth." Ken walked in. "Why do you look deep in

31

thought? Is everything okay?"

Before I said anything, Mom raised the item in her hand. "The doctor prescribed medication for Mimi's high cholesterol."

I gave her a suspicious stare. Why did she understand what Ken said in Mandarin?

"What is it?" Ken took the pill bottle. "Lipitor."

I nodded. "At least now I can eat whatever I want." Directing my gaze toward him, I tried to push aside my qualms. "How is Nancy doing? How many nursing homes did Joseph and you visit today?"

Ken leaned against the quartz countertop. "Nancy's condition has improved. The hospital wants to release her in a few days. Joseph picked the Whitehall of Deerfield. The place is nice. They have an outstanding rehabilitation program."

"I'm glad he decided to place Nancy in a skilled nursing facility." I pursed my lips, dread creeping into my heart once more. Would I make the same decision if presented with a similar situation?

"He still feels guilty that he can't take her home." Ken rubbed his forehead, his tone thoughtful. "But he can't provide her with the care she needs."

"I..." My word hung in the air when Mom tugged at my sleeve to interrupt. "Yes?"

"Aren't you going to the prayer meeting tonight?" She stood up. "Dinner is ready. We just have to reheat the dishes."

I helped her with the microwave while Ken went to fetch Jonny. "Mom, thank you for watching Jonny. Before you came, I couldn't attend the prayer meeting."

She chuckled. "I don't watch Jonny. I play with him."

"You do?" I gaped.

She slid the plate onto the dining table. "We played Monopoly last week."

An appetizing aroma drifted into my nostrils. I looked at the baked chicken and swallowed to avoid drooling. "Nice. Finally, I don't have to eat lettuce and snow pea pods anymore."

Jonny trod into the kitchen. "Hi, Nana. Hi, Mommy."

"Have you done your homework? Nana said she will play Monopoly with you later." I moved over to kiss him. "Out of curiosity, how do you communicate with Nana? You don't speak Taiwanese."

"I speak English, and she responds in Taiwanese." Jonny

shrugged with his usual careless attitude.

"And you understand each other?" I raised my eyebrows.

"Yeah, we do." He wrinkled his nose as if I'd said something stupid.

I muttered, "It's almost like speaking in tongues."

After finishing the last piece of chicken wing, I plopped back in my chair with a grin. "I can never be a vegetarian. How did I survive without meat during the past months?"

I spoke in Mandarin, partly to myself and also to Ken. Mom cast me a puzzled glance, and Jonny shrugged again.

Ken checked his watch. "We'd better go."

Like always, Ken presided over the prayer meeting. We used the ACTS format. At the end, we recited the Lord's Prayer together. Following the loud amen from everyone, I stood up, ready to take leave.

Mark Yang, a brother in his thirties who'd never come to the meeting before, blocked our exit. "Pastor Ken, do you have a few minutes? Can I talk to you in your office?"

I'd been a pastor's wife for over ten years and was used to dealing with unexpected circumstances. Still, I stifled a sigh, sensing a trace of dissatisfaction in my heart.

Lord, please forgive me for my lack of concern for others. I'm edgy because I have to go to work early tomorrow morning.

I took a seat nearby and searched my purse for the cell phone.

Oh no. I didn't bring it with me.

With nothing else to do, I picked up a piece of paper from the recycle bin and jotted down the outline for my next week's Sunday school class.

At last, my husband's footsteps sounded behind me. "Did you call home to let them know we would be out late?"

"I forgot to bring my cell phone." I couldn't avoid the icicles fringing my tone. "Let's go. It's almost ten. Hope Jonny has gone to bed by now."

I intended to ask Ken what he and Mark talked about, but knew well he wouldn't tell me. As a pastor, he took confidentiality seriously.

As the car approached our bungalow, two figures sitting on the front porch came into view. I didn't wait for Ken to pull the car into the garage. "Stop."

I jumped out. The sight made me shudder. Even with his face buried against my mother's knees, my son's howling assaulted my ears. "Mom. Jonny."

Jonny raised his head and sprang into my bosom. "Mommy."

"What's the matter?" I kissed his wet cheek.

"I'm so worried." He wiped his teary eyes with a hand. "I'm so scared."

Mom trod to my side. "You didn't come home at your usual hour. Jonny tried to call Ken but didn't reach him. He insisted something bad must have happened to you both."

"Darling, I'm so sorry." I cringed, my heart aching.

Jonny leaned his head against my shoulder. "What will happen to me if you and Daddy die? Nana is too old to take care of me."

From my experience, he needed emotional support now, not reasoning. I patted his back. "Son, I know. I understand."

Ken came over to take him from my arms. "Jonny, we'll be around. We'll watch you grow up."

After a few long minutes, Jonny's mouth curved up into a grin.

I let out a relieved breath. "Well, let's all go into the house. It's late."

As we were tucking Jonny into the bed, an article I read earlier popped into my mind.

In ancient Rome, when a general who'd just won a victory paraded atop a chariot throughout the capital to receive the public's adoration, a servant stood behind him and kept whispering into his ears, "Memento mori. Remember death."

Seized by fear, plus an unspeakable sadness, I hurried back to our room and grabbed Ken's hand. "Why did Jonny become hysterical tonight? Does my mom look old? Why do humans have to grow old and die?"

"I have no answers for you." He gave my arm a gentle pat. "Go to bed. We have work to do tomorrow."

Chapter Six

Late May 2010

A cramp in my right thigh woke me up. I groaned. The side effects of Lipitor.

I forced myself to sit up. Even after seven hours of rest, fatigue still dogged me. I headed to the bathroom with an unsteady gait.

As I stumbled into the kitchen, Mom, her hair looking grayish under the bright morning sunshine, glanced up from her cereal. "Mimi, did you sleep well? Why do you look exhausted?"

"I'm fine." I contrived a smile. "Has Ken gone to church?"

She returned to her breakfast. "He's just left. As usual, he wants to be there before anyone else."

"Mommy, you got up late today," Jonny chimed in. "You'd better hurry, or I'll be late for my Sunday school lesson."

"Sorry, darling." I pecked his cheek and grabbed a yogurt. "As soon as you and Nana are ready, we can go. I'll eat this in Daddy's office."

Two hours later, the Sunday worship concluded with a benediction from Ken. I got up and strolled to the adult Sunday school classroom for my seekers' class. Two unfamiliar faces had joined the regular attendees.

Must be here for the free meal.

Once in a while, the church organized a potluck lunch to encourage everyone to invite their friends and relatives.

I rubbed my sore leg muscles and let out a low breath, hoping Mom wouldn't indulge in the sweets.

My lesson focused on the godship of Jesus Christ. I flipped to a page in the binder and spoke from my handwritten notes. Afterward, one of the newcomers, a woman named Julia, raised her hand. "Do you know about Falun Gong?"

I nodded.

She folded her arms across her chest, her voice curt. "Li Hongzhi, Falun Gong's leader, declares he is God. Why don't you believe in him but you accept Jesus' claim?"

The room fell silent as all focused on me for a response.

Lord, please give me wisdom. I sucked in a quick breath. "Being a scientist, I try to keep an open mind. If anyone could point to some ancient books that prophesied his coming, and if he was also willing to die for my sin, then I will take a serious look at him."

Julia squinted. "Where are the prophecies about Jesus?"

I checked my notes. "According to studies, more than three hundred prophecies from the Old Testament were fulfilled in Jesus Christ."

She cocked her head. "How do you know those were not inserted into the Old Testament by Jesus' disciples?"

"Good question." I fiddled with my pen to calm down. "Have you heard about the Dead Sea Scrolls? They're considered among the most significant archeological finds of the twentieth century. Except for the book of Esther, all the other Old Testament books were there. Experts have dated many of them to be at least 100 BCE, long before Jesus was born. When one compares those manuscripts with the editions we have now, the difference is negligible, less than one percent."

Julia's face dropped. She pushed against the desk to stand up, then walked out.

Oh no. My heart sank. Had I offended her?

Mrs. Yang, an elderly lady who came from Mainland China to visit her son, sat on my left. She leaned over to pat my arm. "Julia is a member of Falun Gong. Your answers are to the point. I hope she'll take them into consideration."

The class bell rang. I I summoned a strained smile. "Well, time for our potluck."

Instead of going to lunch, I roamed the church building in search of Julia but didn't find her. My words must have made her so angry she relinquished her claim to a sumptuous meal.

With a weight on my spirit, I plodded into the dining hall—where my mother held a plate piled high with desserts. I rushed over, my fingers twitching around my purse strap. "Mom."

"Problem?" She took a few steps away from me.

"Yes, problem." I gestured to the plate with my free hand. "All of these—"

She held up a finger. "Don't start."

I trekked after her. "Don't start what?"

She quickened her steps. "You know what I'm talking about."

I gritted my teeth and ran to snag a piece of cookie from her plate.

She raised her voice. "Can you take it easy for once, please?"

People nearby directed their eyes toward us. Mom shot me a hard glance and went to sit by Ken.

My husband pinched the bridge of his nose, then gave me a dismissive wave. "Go get some food."

I clenched my hands, my fingernails biting into my skin. Mom's pupils were so blown I could see them from where I stood. My shoulders slumped. "I'm glad we drove two cars to church this morning. I'm leaving now. Mom and Jonny can ride with you."

Back at home, I sank into the tan sofa and scowled at my plants beneath the bay window, a weariness permeating both my body and mind. Why couldn't Mom control herself? *Oh, Lord, what will I do if something bad happens to her?*

An hour passed. The sound of our garage door rumbling open snapped me out of my thoughts.

Mom charged into the living room and pointed at me. "How dare you talk to me like that at church? You made me lose face in front of everyone."

I sat up from the sofa with some difficulties. "Is face more important than health?"

"It's *my* health!"

Ken, standing behind my mother, glared at me.

Great. Even my husband didn't think I did it out of love for Mom.

A lump lodged in my throat. I swallowed hard. "You're committing suicide. I won't let you kill yourself."

Ken shook his head and left with Jonny for the basement.

"It's my life. I can do whatever I want." Mom bared her teeth, her nostrils flaring.

I cracked my knuckles. "Your life isn't your own. It's from God. You need to be a good steward to take care of what God has entrusted to you."

She swept an arm across the space between us. "How about you? Are you following the biblical teachings to talk to your mother like that?"

I rubbed my temple. "You're dodging the issue again."

"I'm not. I deserve respect from my daughter, not nagging. You haven't changed a bit, still grumpy and self-righteous all the time."

Heat flushing through my body, I remained silent.

"You know why I didn't care to go to church with you before? I didn't see your Christian faith having any impact on you. You went to church and studied the Bible, but your behaviors and values didn't change. I encouraged you to go shopping with girls from your church, and you scowled at 'such juvenile pursuits.' You couldn't trust others and were full of anger. Although I believed in our folk religion, I handled our situation better than you did."

I winced, stung by Mom's icy tone. A regretful memory intruded as I sank deeper against the sofa's squashy cushions.

A few days following my baptism, Jo-May, a classmate, approached me after a difficult exam. "How did it go? Will you get an A like before?"

I'd sniggered. "Why does it have anything to do with you? It's none of your business."

She paled as if shocked by my reply. Then her jaw tightened, and her eyes narrowed. "There's no need to be so rude. I'm just trying to be friendly." She left without another word.

My shoulders stiffened. *Was it true? After so many years, had I not changed?*

I wiped away my perspiration with a Kleenex.

Time for a different approach. Dropping my arm, I charged ahead. "I have a PhD degree in biochemistry and work in a pharmaceutical company. From my studies, I know diabetes is a serious disease. You ought to control your body weight and watch your diet."

Mom lowered her brows, the tendons standing out in her neck. "Just because you're a doctor and I'm a high school graduate, you can tell me what to do? If I didn't force you to stay at Ohio State University to complete the program, you would have given up and gone to Hong Kong to become a housewife, a good-for-nothing nobody like me."

My skin tingled with new sweat on my forehead. I shot back. "So, without you, I wouldn't have received my degree? Don't forget you didn't give me any financial support. I got a scholarship."

"Oh yeah? Who gave life to whom? Who took care of you when you were sick? Who comforted you when you were hurt? Who gave you the time to study to earn that scholarship?"

"Please..." I tried to stand up. But a spasm hit my muscles, and I fell off the sofa.

Mom hurried toward me. "Mimi, are you all right?"

I massaged my leg, yet the pain didn't subside.

Her arms fluttered as she hovered. "What's the matter? Are you ill?"

"It's the side effect of Lipitor."

She stooped over me. "You need to see the doctor. Maybe she can prescribe another medication."

"I will." I clasped her offered hand to sit up. "Mom, I'm worried about your diabetes. Please try to control your diet."

My words stirred up her emotions again, and she yanked her hand away. "You're a control freak. I come here to enjoy life with you. I don't need to be told what I can or can't do."

My legs throbbed. I tried to talk but couldn't.

"Mimi, does it hurt?" She pulled me into her bosom. "You must see the doctor."

I leaned on her shoulder and sensed the pain easing. "Dr. Stone is hard to make an appointment with. She won't see me right away just because of this little problem. We're leaving for our cruise vacation on Saturday. I'll call her tomorrow morning and hope to see her soon."

"Are you sure?" Mom eased back and brushed my hair away from my face. "Can our trip be rescheduled?"

"No. Anyhow, muscle soreness is an expected side effect, not a big deal." I sat up from her. "Look, I feel better already. Time to prepare dinner."

"Let me cook." She let go of me and hurried away to the kitchen.

I slouched on the sofa. Why didn't my good intentions have good outcomes?

I shut my eyes to calm down, yet the dread that had gripped me after Dad's passing refused to lift. My mind conjured up an image of my mother and me sharing the same bed and how fear prompted me to monitor her breathing during her sleep.

"Dinner is ready."

Mom's loud call snapped me out of my thoughts. Wow, how long had I sat there brooding? This had to stop. *Lord, thank You for my mother. Please give me wisdom so I can help her improve her health.*

I walked over to survey the plates: steamed fish with ginger and green onion, spicy chicken, and spinach sautéed with garlic.

The sight made my mouth water. "Looks super delicious. How did you manage to whip up three beautiful dishes in such a short time? You're great."

Beaming, Mom flashed me a smile. "Don't you know I learned to cook when I was six?"

I rolled my eyes. The drama queen was exaggerating again.

Chapter Seven

Mom and I left Chicago early in the morning on Saturday and arrived at the port of Miami by noon. As soon as we stepped on the ship for our seven-day cruise, she pulled me to the restaurant. "Wow, shrimp scampi. I wish Ken and Jonny were here with us. They both love shrimp."

"Haven't I told you before? Unlike you, they hate cruises and prefer to stay home." I swallowed to resist the urge to roll my eyes. "Mom, remember not to eat too many desserts."

She frowned and shut her mouth tight.

I stifled a groan, unsure whether I'd made the right decision to take a cruise with my mother.

After the mandatory muster drill, we sauntered around to get acquainted with our surroundings.

In the gym, I pointed to the treadmill. "Let's come here to exercise later today."

She glanced at my legs. "Can you? Aren't your muscles still sore?"

"Not completely normal yet. But I'm determined to work out, anyway. Would you like to join me?"

Before she responded, a woman about my mom's age walked over and shouted in Taiwanese, "Are you Toshiko?"

Mom turned around, her jaw slackening and eyes widening. "Are you...?" Then she took a step forward. "Jasmine?"

"It's me, your old neighbor." The woman took Mom's hand and gave it an enthusiastic shake.

Head tipped to one side, I stood back a pace—waiting. Mom rarely talked about her past. When I was a child, she used to take me to her parents' house to see my grandpa. Auntie Su-Hua once told me that Mom's mother died young. Her father remarried, and her stepmother bore four children.

Soon after I started elementary school, my grandfather passed away. Afterward, Mom never returned to her previous home, although my uncle and three aunts, her half brother and sisters, often came to our house to visit.

An older Caucasian gentleman with a slightly hunched back appeared. "Jasmine, ready to go?"

Jasmine let go of my mother's hand. "This is my husband, Liam."

After she made the introduction, we exchanged our cabin numbers.

"Sorry, I need to go now. We have a date with some friends." Before she left, she touched Mom's arm. "The captain's night is tomorrow. Do you want to go to the salon with me early in the morning?"

Mom nodded. While they strolled away, she murmured, "I wonder why she married a foreigner. Does she speak English?"

A whistle blasted.

I grasped her fingers. "The ship is about to leave. Let's go upstairs to view the harbor."

"What's there to see?" She fluffed her hair, mussy from the trip and showing white at its roots. "Haven't we seen enough?"

Mom had seemed cheerful a moment ago. Why did her mood change? Could it have something to do with meeting an old neighbor?

My interest level soared.

***

While waiting for Mom to return from the salon the next day, I scanned the daily newsletter for things to do.

"Not bad." I squinted at the enticing program. Dance lessons, jewelry talks, and bridge games. I settled on the tour of the engine control room.

I didn't expect to see Liam there. "I'm Ruth." I approached with my palm out to shake. "Remember me? We met at the gym yesterday."

"Ah, yes." He took my hand, then patted it with his other one. "Beautiful young lady, the daughter of Jasmine's old friend."

With his cheeks rounding up under twinkling green eyes, he seemed like a jolly fellow. I soon learned that he and Jasmine had come here to celebrate their tenth wedding anniversary.

After the tour, we returned to the deck.

Liam leaned against the guardrail. "All night, my wife raved about her past with your mother."

"Really?" I peeked at the cafeteria nearby. "Do you have time? Would you like to have tea together?"

He checked his watch. "All right. They won't get their hair done until after eleven, anyway."

Inside the cozy cafeteria with its soft elevator music, I made a cup of my favorite tea. The sweet aroma of cinnamon mixed with vanilla drifted into my nostrils. "What did Jasmine say about my mother?"

He poured sugar into his coffee, then added creamer. "She told me Toshiko has an unusual story."

My heartbeat skittered. Was I holding my breath? "Why so?"

"Your mother never told you?" He sipped his coffee. "Before I tell you what I've learned, I'm curious why your mom moved to Japan."

Sinking back against the padded fabric chair, I tipped my face up at the recessed lighting and resisted the urge to roll my neck back and forth to release the immediate tension now claiming my muscles. "I received a scholarship from Ohio State University to study biochemistry in their PhD program. I would have stayed in Taiwan, but at that time, Taiwan's biochemical research was rather limited. Most of my classmates went abroad to continue their graduate studies. One month before I departed for Columbus, Mom's application for a job at the Isetan Departmental Store in Tokyo had gone through. I left for the US two days after her flight to Japan."

Liam inclined his head. "I see."

No, I didn't tell him the whole story. Back then, my mom and I seldom talked about my future. Maybe we weren't prepared to face the conclusion from such a discussion. When I mustered up my courage and asked Mom what she would do if I went to the US, she told me not to worry and urged me to do whatever I needed to do.

I sucked in a deep breath to control my emotions, savoring the tea's calming scent. "Now tell me what you know about my mother."

He pulled back his shoulders, his polo shirt stretching out over his bulging belly. "Jasmine said the two families had always lived next to each other, but she never saw Toshiko until she was ten. She's a bit older than your mom."

What? How was that possible? I nearly splashed my tea on my favorite teal silk blouse that I snapped up from the Salvation Army last year. "What's going on?"

"Toshiko didn't live with her father in her early years."

I blurted out, "Why?"

"Jasmine said after Toshiko's mother died, her father remarried and sent her to live with her grandmother." Liam's nose scrunched and his green eyes dimmed.

An old yellowed photo popped into my mind. My mom, still a toddler, snuggled in her grandma's arms, both beaming bright smiles.

Yet, Mom never mentioned that she lived with her grandma for so many years.

"Jasmine said she would never forget the first time she met your mother." Liam scratched his chin. "An autumn afternoon in southern Taiwan. She was skipping rope by the door when an unfamiliar girl joined her. The two of them jumped together in perfect harmony for a while. Then they stopped and laughed aloud."

I couldn't help chuckling at the image of two children sharing a rope.

Liam blinked a few times, and his voice dropped. "Unfortunately, the good times didn't last. Soon your mother became a free maid in the family. She not only took care of her younger siblings but also had to cook, do laundry, and clean the house. She had no chance to play with Jasmine anymore."

A wave of emotions—anger, disbelief, and grief—flooded my heart. I lowered my cup of tea to the table, not trusting my hands to keep it steady.

How did Mom handle all those chores as a nine-year-old? Did

her stepmother abuse her?

Liam braced his elbows on the table, coffee cup held between both hands by his mouth. Over its brim, his eyes gleamed. "Jasmine admired your mom. She shouldered the responsibilities like an adult. Not only that, she continued to do well at school."

Grandpa, as a teacher, put great emphasis on a child's education. Mom must have gone all out at school to win his approval.

Didn't he know about the abuses? The woman I called Grandma usually spoke in an authoritative tone. Perhaps Grandpa had been afraid of her.

While I kept quiet, Liam finished his coffee, then stood up. "I almost forgot. I need to run an errand with a front desk agent. Miss Ruth, nice to chat with you. Talk to you later."

Watching him leave, I pondered what my mother had endured. Moisture clouded my eyes.

Nine years old, the age of my son. Jonny often cried for nothing, like a spoiled child. How about me? At nine, I didn't behave any better. Yet at that age, my mom had no choice but to work like an adult.

The next day was still a sea day. Mom and I indulged in the Roman Spa. We enjoyed a light meal, then went with a woman named Lisa to a room full of instruments.

Pressing her palm to the jade broach on her blouse, Mom glanced at the exit. "What is this for?"

"Are you nervous? Don't worry." I grasped her hand. "She'll do a whole-body tissue analysis for us."

The results came out right away, and Lisa faced my mother. "Your daughter has perfect scores. But your fat index is too high. You need to eat fewer carbohydrates and exercise more."

When I translated for Mom, she pursed her lips.

Lisa herded us to the pool, and we did a round of aqua aerobics until another girl announced we could go to the massage area.

After I lay down, she smeared a layer of oil mixed with sand over my back and rubbed my skin with force. "This is effective for removing dead cells."

Full bodywork from my feet and all the way to my scalp followed.

Mom lay on a bed next to me. "So enjoyable."

Letting out any remaining tension, I turned my head toward her.

"Not over yet. Up next is the sauna and steam room treatment."

Six hours later, I returned to our cabin with Mom, my whole person flabby, relaxed.

I took the skipping rope out of the drawer. "The massage was beneficial. The Lipitor side effects seem gone. Shall we go to the gym?"

"Are you nuts? Why do you bring a rope to the cruise?" She stood up. "I only want to have some fun."

I decided to ride a stationary bike with Mom. "I met Jasmine's husband yesterday. He said you lived with your grandmother until you were nine. Why didn't you mention it before?"

She didn't answer and stomped down on the pedals harder.

Hmm. "Liam also said your stepmother abused you."

"Enough. Let's go." She stopped her pedaling.

We trod back in silence. The knot in my stomach clenched tighter every minute. But why? Why was I flustered with so many emotions?

Should I let go of what Liam had told me? An urgent desire to know more about my mother prompted me to open my mouth. "Mom..."

She waved a hand, her colored-glass ring glaring from her finger. "I need to take a walk. Go to dinner by yourself. I'll eat at the buffet upstairs."

At the door's click, my mom's testimony after her baptism in Columbus, Ohio, rushed into my mind. "Although I used to be empty, the Lord has brought me back full. I chose Naomi as my baptismal name because my life is a testimony that God can change 'Mara' into 'Naomi.'"

Mom had reversed what Naomi said in the book of Ruth.

Mara meant bitter, and Naomi meant sweet. Now I understood why.

Someone knocked.

"Who is that?" I twisted my errant watch face into view. Almost dinnertime.

"Me." My mom's voice sounded. Didn't she say she would go to the buffet on the upper deck? "I forgot my key card."

I let her in. "Will you come to dinner with me?"

"Yes, lest you worry about me eating too many sweets." Her sheepish grin warmed my heart, like Jonny's so often did. "Plus, tomorrow we'll join the excursions. I have to get ready."

Over the next few days, we had excursions every morning. In St. Thomas, we went on a fish-watching submarine tour with Liam and Jasmine. We signed up for a rainforest tour in the Dominican Republic. In Nassau, I took a bus tour with my mother around the island.

Back in our cabin at night, I intended to talk to her, but she put her manicured hands on her waist and said, "I'm so tired. Let's do it later."

At the Miami airport, Mom dragged her fingers through her hair, fluffing the freshly dyed-black strands. "What a wonderful vacation. I'm so pleased to have run into Jasmine."

"Did you two exchange phone numbers and addresses?" How could I broach her past?

"Yes. She lives in Miami." Mom beamed, sinking back into the uncomfortable waiting chair. "Maybe they'll come to visit us soon."

I stared at her. "We have a whole hour before boarding. Tell me what happened when you were a child."

Her smile disappeared. "You're such a strong-willed and persistent brat."

"Like you." I scrunched my nose to tease her.

She heaved a sigh. "So long ago. I've forgotten most of it."

I nudged her arm with mine. "Tell me why you went back to live with your father and stepmother. Liam said you stayed with your nana since you were a baby."

A distant expression glazed her eyes. "My nana passed away when I was nine."

I scratched my cheek, debating whether to continue.

Too late.

Mom's shoulders slumped, and she leaned into me. "Nana loved me very much. She knew she wouldn't live to see me grow up. To prepare me for an uncertain future, she trained me to cook and do house chores as soon as I reached six."

I conjured up a picture in my head. An old woman with bound feet helped a girl chop meat in the kitchen, and her childish giggles lilted through the air.

A lump lodged in my heart.

"I was still not fully prepared." Mom tipped her head against mine. With her so close, I could feel the weight of her next breath.

47

"The first time my stepmother asked me to sweep the floor, I missed a piece of crumpled paper in the corner. Guess what she did?"

My stomach clenched. I closed my eyes, unsure of what stirred inside of me.

"She"—Mom's voice shook—"stuck the trash into my mouth and forced me to swallow it."

My mouth went dry, heat swelling my throat. An angel, the apple of her nana's eye, fell from heaven to hell in a matter of days.

"After that, I never made the same mistake." A wry laugh shook her body as she pushed herself away from me. "For my tenth birthday, my dad bought me a cake. But I didn't get to taste it. My stepmother gave it to her own children."

What! I jerked farther away from her. "Why didn't your father do something?"

She shrugged and dipped her chin.

With a trembling hand, I grasped her arm. "That's why you can't resist sweets?"

The PA system called our flight. Mom stood and smoothed her rumpled slacks. "Time to board. Let's go."

I followed her to our seats. She shut her eyes and slept through the flight while my shoulders stiffened and my chest tightened.

Chapter Eight

After our cruise vacation, I paid Dr. Stone another visit. She prescribed Vytorin, a new cholesterol drug from our company. A month on the medication without any major problems convinced me the side effects seemed mild, although my muscles were sore most days.

On a Saturday morning in early July, I woke up from a nightmare packed with battle scenes. My whole body hurt as if a thousand spears had pierced me. For almost an hour, I lay still and prayed the pain would go away.

At last, I swung out of bed, groaning aloud. "Ken, I'm running a fever. My muscles and bones ache like crazy."

While I stumbled down on the scratchy beige carpet, he retrieved the thermometer and placed it under my tongue. After the device beeped, he examined it. "You don't have a fever—97.8."

"But I feel like fiery heat is attacking me." I moaned again.

He touched my forehead. "Not hot at all."

"Must be the side effects of Vytorin. Something is seriously wrong." My voice cracked as the cramp continued.

"Let me call Dr. Stone." He hurried away.

When he returned, he sank to his knees beside me. His hands brought cold comfort to my shoulders. "Dr. Stone said to stop Vytorin right away. If you develop other symptoms today, I'll have

49

to take you to the emergency room." He helped me get back to bed. "Take it easy. Let's pray for no other complications."

I rubbed my temple. "Jonny's piano lesson is at nine, followed by his martial arts class. Could you drive him over?"

"Of course." Ken's affectionate pat jostled my shoulder. "You haven't had breakfast, right? How about a bowl of cereal?"

While I was eating, Jonny walked in. "Mommy, are you all right?"

"Don't worry." I forced a smile. "I'm better already. Are you leaving with Daddy soon?"

He hugged me and kissed my cheek. "I love you. I'll pray for you."

His sweet words brought warmth to my heart. I kissed him back. "Thank you, darling. You're such a kind and considerate boy."

Jonny grinned and scrambled away.

With food in my stomach, the pain eased slightly.

After Ken and Jonny left, Mom came to sit by me with a cup of honey water. "How are you feeling? Any other symptoms?"

"Luckily, no." I grasped the cup.

"Why is this drug so powerful? Can you not take it?" Her fingers brushed my forehead, whisking aside my bangs and sweeping me back into childhood.

"The doctor told me to stop." The recent problematic development in my company flashed across my mind. "It's never-ending. One difficulty after another."

She touched my chin and tipped my face toward hers. "Why did you say that?"

"No particular reason." I swallowed hard, not wanting to alarm her with my work issues.

"Don't lie. Something in your tone doesn't sound right." Her hand dropped to my shoulder. "What is it? Is it related to your job?"

Wow. She had a sharp sixth sense.

"You don't want to talk about it?" She gave me a gentle pat. "Bring it to the Lord. Remember what happened when you applied to the graduate schools in the US?"

Why did Mom bring up the past? Did she worry my pride would jeopardize my job like it almost ruined my chance to study abroad?

Maybe she noticed that, back then, I not only shunned away from interacting with others but also donned an enormous ego as my survival mechanism. To apply for scholarships from US universities, I put together eight applications to topflight schools, including Harvard, Cornell, and Princeton. I was prideful and confident I would receive several positive replies.

Did she know what happened?

I let out a wry laugh. "What do you know about that?"

"No school accepted you in your first round of application, and you became upset." A tiny frown creased Mom's forehead. "I forgot what you did next. Did you go talk to Dr. Lu?"

"Yeah." I brushed aside a stray wisp of hair. "I became confused and asked Dr. Lu how to seek God's will. She told me that the first place she went to was the Scriptures and asked what I'd been reading recently. I'd just studied Gideon in Judges."

"Ah, I'm familiar with the Gideon story." Mom lifted her gaze toward the ceiling. "God called him to lead the Israelites to fight against the Midianites. So, he gathered thirty-two thousand men. God told him that if they won, Israel would claim glory for herself. In the end, only three hundred soldiers went with him, and they won the battle."

"Unbelievable." I reached out to touch her arm. "You study your Bible well."

"I'm a pastor's mother-in-law. I need to know the Bible." Her lips curled into a cheeky grin. "What did Dr. Lu say?"

"She helped me understand I couldn't accomplish anything without God. With her encouragement, I sent out another five applications." I sipped the water. A sweet, savory flavor danced on my taste buds. Was it the Manuka honey we bought from Costco?

Mom helped me put the cup on the nightstand. "Didn't a school in Texas offer you a scholarship? But you decided not to take it."

"Ha, I'm glad you remember. You yelled at me, 'You have to accept it. You're lucky to even have something.'"

She ducked her head, the grin turning sheepish. "You gave me such a weird reason. You said, 'I believe God in His King's style will give me a scholarship to Ohio State University, the best among the five.'"

Did I say that? Yet I remembered what'd happened next. The deadline to make a decision approached, and I mailed my acceptance letter to Texas.

Two days later, a man from Ohio State University called and

offered me a scholarship for the PhD program in biochemistry. Since it was so late in the process, he needed my reply right away. Ecstatic, I responded with a yes on the spot.

I narrowed my eyes and wagged a finger at Mom. "After our run-in, I might have stopped sharing information with you. Do you know I walked down a path packed with twists and turns?"

"Really?" Her eyebrows spiked up. "Tell me."

"I sent a telegram to Texas to inform them I planned to go to Ohio State University. After a few weeks, instead of obtaining an I-20, the form required for a student visa application, I received a letter from OSU, saying that they couldn't accept me anymore because a university in Texas had threatened to take them to court. The news shocked me. Why didn't they allow me to change my choice?"

She bobbed her head. "You mentioned something to me."

I scratched my cheek. "I turned to God. A Bible verse emerged in my head. 'My ears had heard of You but now my eyes have seen You.' I lifted a prayer, 'Lord, my lack of faith in You is the root problem. I'll learn to trust and obey.' After I prayed, a peace enveloped my whole being as if I spoke face-to-face with the living God."

Mom stared at me, waiting for me to continue.

"Another letter from Texas reached me. The school decided to increase my stipend. When I broke the news to you and said I would decline the offer, you gawked and screamed, 'You're insane. OSU doesn't want you, and Texas offers you more money. How can you not take it?'"

I rubbed the back of my neck, my body stiffening all over again.

Mom scooted closer to hug me. "I wish I had become a Christian earlier. My values would have been different. I wouldn't have worried so much."

My heart softened, and my muscles loosened up. "You always have my best interest in mind."

"Mimi, thank you for saying that." She ran her fingers through my hair. "How did it work out at the end?"

"I received a note from OSU, advising me to obtain a release from the other school, and they could still accept me. At last, I went to OSU."

My mouth crinkled up as I thought of my first day at Ohio State University. When I stepped into my departmental office, the secretary exclaimed, "So, you're that girl from Taiwan who almost got us sued. It's the first in our history!"

I grasped Mom's arm. "I appreciate you reminding me of our shared past full of challenges. So many things are beyond our control. We can only put them in God's hands."

She squinted. "So, is your company laying you off?"

"No." I wiggled back deeper into the pillows propping me up, the slipcover's soft fabric sticky against my terrycloth robe. "But our project got canceled, and they'll transfer my whole group to a different division."

She relaxed her shoulders. "Well, at least you still have a job."

How could she dismiss it so easily? Heat flared through me again. "You don't understand. I spent *six* years in the field. We've done a lot of outstanding work."

Mom kept quiet. Did my harsh tone hurt her feelings? Oops.

I reached for her hand, pained by her somber expression. "I shouldn't have raised my voice. What's on your mind?"

"I used to know a lot about your life." She lowered her chin, her fingers twitchy beneath mine. "I'm getting old. A lot of happenings are out of my comprehension now."

I bit my lip. "Please don't say that. Why do you insist on keeping your apartment in Tokyo and only visiting from time to time? It'd be like before if you lived here with us."

"It can never be like before. But I'm glad you're settled with a husband and a son. Both of them are so kindhearted." Her tone was gentle like the morning ray.

The clock struck ten, and she stood. "I'd better go prepare lunch."

"Thank you." I brought a palm to my face, grateful I didn't have to drag my sore body out of bed to cook. What would I do without her?

The phone rang. Mom answered and conversed in rapid Taiwanese. *Must be Auntie Jane from Philadelphia.*

I lay still and eavesdropped.

After the clock rang out twelve times, Mom walked in. "Mimi, lunch is ready."

I directed my gaze at her. "Are Ken and Jonny home?"

"Ken said he would take Jonny to McDonald's, then to the library. Can you get up? Or do you want to have lunch in bed?"

Humm. I hadn't eaten in bed for a long while. "Will you eat with

53

me here?"

"Sure." She hurried away and brought back a tray with two plates.

I sat up. "Who called? Auntie Jane?"

She tucked a napkin around my neck. "She invited me to visit her."

I straightened the pillows behind me and sat up against them. "How is she?"

"Very well. Super busy, though." Mom beamed. "Did I tell you, when the housing market dipped in the 1980s, she quit her engineering job and became an investor in rental properties? She's rich."

"Yeah. You told me many times already." I brought a hand to my mouth and feigned a yawn. "Why are you so proud of your sisters' accomplishments? Aren't they your stepmother's children?"

She grinned. "I was like their second mother."

I sucked in a quick breath. Right. She almost single-handedly raised her siblings.

How did she let go of her resentment and express only kindness toward her rivals?

"Every time you come to Chicago, Auntie Jane asks you to go see her. Will you go this year?" I sampled the egg foo young. It tasted sweet. I glared at Mom. "Did you add sugar?"

"This dish needs sugar to be right. I put in a tiny bit." She let out a sheepish grin. "No, I won't visit her this year. I'm concerned about your health and plan to stay here with you."

Let it be. What she told me at the Miami airport popped up in my head. "I've been wondering..."

My words got lost on the tip of my tongue. How should I frame my question so I didn't offend her?

"Yes?" She took a bite of the pork chop.

I pushed the green beans around with my chopsticks. "Your stepmother mistreated you so badly. Have you ever felt resentful toward your siblings?"

She chewed faster.

I studied her face. "From how Uncle and Aunties interact with you, I guess you must have treated them well when they were young. How did you do it when their mother abused you?"

Mom swallowed her food. "They were only a bunch of innocent

54

kids. They had nothing to do with their mother's behavior."

Her chopsticks plucked a bite from her plate, then let it drop. She pointed them at me. "Remember I told you my nana loved me very much? Her love remains with me even today. When your heart is full of love, there's no room left for inferior emotions."

Wow. My mouth slid open. "You spoke like a wise philosopher."

"No, I'm not." Laughing, she set her chopsticks back to work. "I'm only your mother."

As the light of her love shone on me, my heart warmed.

A Bible verse that had long bothered me popped up. "Her many sins have been forgiven—for she loved much."

I often wondered whether Luke had misquoted Jesus' words in Chapter 7 of his Gospel book. Shouldn't it make more sense to say, "Her many sins have been forgiven so that she loved much"?

No, Luke quoted the Lord's words correctly.

Jesus must be so full of the love from His heavenly Father that, even dying on the cross, He could proclaim, "Father, forgive them, because they do not know what they are doing."

Mom's forehead puckered, and her chopsticks stilled. "Plus, as time went by, my stepmother treated me better and better. I suppose in the beginning she was jealous of my father's love for me. When I proved not to be a big threat, she relaxed."

"You're so forgiving." I reached out to touch her shoulder.

"I'm practical. If I refuse to forgive, I'm still a hostage to the person who's hurt me. To set myself free, I have to let go of my enmity." She cast me a meaningful glance. "I'm worried about you. I sense you still harbor deep resentments toward your aunt Su-Hua."

Auntie Su-Hua! I sank my chopsticks into my plate. "Let's finish lunch. Food is getting cold."

Chapter Nine

The Vytorin scare prompted Dr. Stone to give me another cholesterol medication, Crestor. In addition, she worried the drug might have damaged my heart muscle, so she sent me to a cardiologist.

Inside Dr. Jonsson's office the next day, the nurse placed sticky patches on my chest, legs, and arms. "We'll do a stress test first."

The treadmill started at a slow pace, then picked up in speed. Soon, I was huffing and puffing.

After I stopped, Dr. Jonsson smiled. "Your heart function is normal. You don't need any further procedures."

Whew! Great. Now I just needed to make sure Crestor didn't have side effects like the other two.

"'Trust and obey, for there's no other way to be happy in Jesus, but to trust and obey'..." While humming the tune to myself, I stepped into our kitchen.

"Mommy, you're back." Jonny dropped his ice cream bowl and ran to hug me.

I kissed him in return. "Where's Nana?"

"In the backyard."

Standing by the French door, I gripped the cool glass handle while Mom bent to pluck leaves from the sweet potato plants she'd grown from cuttings. A lawn mower rumbled next door, and the fresh-cut-grass scent drifted over the fence.

"What're you looking at?" Jonny's voice rose behind me.

"Nothing." I opened the door and stepped into the pleasant early evening, still hot after the day. "Nana may need me. Let me go help her harvest the greens."

I walked toward Mom. How did she learn to grow sweet potato leaves?

She straightened up and kneaded her lower back. "You're home early. I thought you would stay late to make up for your time off. Nice. Tonight, we'll have stir-fry veggies."

"Wow, quite a lot." I checked the leaves in her basket. "You grew up in the city. Did you learn to garden from Dad?"

"I did." Her fingers brushed against mine. "I never grew anything before I married him. Your dad loved outdoor activities and filled our garden with different plants."

I breathed in deep, thinking of our many plum trees. In early spring, branches full of white flowers swayed in the breeze, and the sweet fragrance swirled around us. "You used to sing a Japanese folk song about flowers. What is it called?"

"Sakura." She raised her face upward.

My gaze followed hers to the fluffy white clouds dotting the blue sky. The summer sun still lingered on the western skyline. "Ah, the cherry blossoms. Do you still know how to sing it?"

"Sakura, sakura, noyama mo..." Mom's crooning floated in the air.

I raked my hair. "Why did Dad know Mandarin, but you didn't?"

A tiny smile tugged at Mom's mouth. "I'm a homemaker. Your dad worked in a bank and had no choice but to learn Mandarin. Plus, his fondness for music helped. He could differentiate tones and intonations easily."

"Dad was an excellent singer." Warmth crept up into my heart. My dad used to organize a band with some relatives who were good at different instruments. Every Saturday evening, the group gathered in our yard and sang various Taiwanese folk songs.

"He often sang 'Green Island Serenade,' a song about a political prisoner exiled to Green Island moaning for his lost love." Mom rubbed her arm, streaking her skin with a smudge of dirt. "The world we grew up in was hostile. Even when you were growing up, it didn't get any easier. In the earliest years of your life, you spoke only our local dialect. It came as a total shock that, on your first day at elementary school, the teacher demanded you to speak Mandarin. You didn't speak a word."

"You still remember?" I put a hand on my hip.

"You came home in tears. Your dad saw you cry and gave you a crash course." She touched her chest. "But you were smart. You ranked number three in your class of about thirty students."

I chuckled. At the end of the first semester, our teacher gave each of us a report card. I saw the number three on mine and hid it away. Mom asked me a few days later where my report card was. I couldn't hide it anymore. To my surprise, she seemed quite pleased. "Funny you mentioned that. I didn't know until then that three wasn't a bad number at all."

Mom massaged her waist. "You always did well at school."

"Are you okay?" I patted her back.

"Oh, my old bones." She grimaced.

My smile slipped away. "You shouldn't bend down for too long. Maybe you need to exercise more."

Her chin jerked up. "Here you go again."

I scratched my cheek. Time to change the subject. "You and Dad were from different parts of Taiwan. How did you two meet?"

She took a step back. "Why do you want to know?"

"Just out of curiosity."

Mom looked down at her feet, digging the toe of her loafer into the soft soil. "Unlike you, in my generation, marriages were often arranged by parents between families with similar economic or educational backgrounds."

I sucked in a quick breath. How did I not know this about my parents? "Did you have any say in the matter?"

She dug her toe deeper, unearthing a worm. "At that time, I tried everything to get away from my stepmother. I wished to continue my education in Taipei to become a nurse. But I had no money."

My gaze fell on the huge cucumber vine at the edge of the yard. "So, marriage became your only opportunity to escape?"

"Yes." She dipped her chin.

"Wasn't it risky? I suppose you hardly knew Dad before you married him."

"Not any riskier than marriages nowadays." She wiggled her brows. "You told me your colleague's story. Helen, right?"

How did Mom remember all my friends' names?

"Didn't she and her husband date for seven years? She never knew his abusive nature until after the wedding." Mom palmed her forehead, then smoothed back her already smooth hair. While I kept silent, she let out an audible breath. "It turned out well. Your dad was a wonderful man."

I patted her hand. "People in our village respected Dad. They often came to our house, arguing in front of him."

Her mouth curved up. "You asked me once, 'What's going on? Why are those angry people talking to Dad?' And I assured you that folks trusted your dad and thought he could help them solve their problems."

"Dad spent lots of time and effort serving others." I picked up the basket for Mom. "But he found opportunities to involve me in his daily life. I still have a picture of me sitting on his shoulder."

Mom threw her head back and laughed with her whole body. "Your dad loved to lift you to his shoulder."

"What's so funny?" I feigned annoyance. Yet deep down, I detected a tenderness spreading through me as I conjured up the image of how Dad, Mom, and I worked together in our yard. "I suppose Dad fueled my lifelong interest in music and gardening."

She stopped laughing, her obvious joy fading beneath a shadowy expression. "Sometimes I wish your dad were still alive. He spoke Mandarin. He would have many things to share with Ken."

I kneaded my brows. "Recently, I've been wondering what went wrong with Dad's surgery. We never questioned that his death might be the result of medical malpractice. Also, why did we lose the house you and Dad built?"

"I don't understand it, either. Your grandpa had connections with local authorities. Rumor has it that he engaged in dishonorable deals with them. I was ignorant, and you were too young." She sighed. "Your father's death and what your aunt and grandpa did afterward dealt you a heavy blow. When you were in college, you never dated. I worried you would turn into a spinster."

That might have worried her, but I'd wanted it. "God intervened."

She dabbed her eyes with her fingers. "I'm grateful He did. Ken is a kind man. Only he can put up with your quirkiness."

I almost blurted out, "Then why did you object to my courtship with Ken in Columbus?"

Words stuck in my throat. She didn't like Ken solely because she couldn't communicate with him. I got her blessing only after I insisted I wouldn't marry anyone else.

It would do no good to talk about that. I swallowed hard. "What do you mean? I'm perfectly normal."

Her short-lived smile faded. "Except that you won't let Ken buy anything unless it's on sale or he has a coupon. And you have wild mood swings."

Wow. Was that how others viewed me?

"So, all the merits belong to Ken?" I made a silly face with crossed eyes. "Aren't you glad I didn't heed your advice to go out with others?"

"You didn't date. Period."

At her subdued response, I tilted my chin with a grin. "I didn't like Ken in the beginning, either."

"You never told me how you two met." She nudged us toward the metal lawn chairs, then sank onto one with a little grunt.

"You never asked."

"Okay, I want to know." She patted the nearby chair for me to join her. "Tell me."

Should I tell my mother that part of my past? I shifted the basket to my other hip, not sure I wanted to settle in for this conversation. Well, she didn't hesitate to share the details about how she married Dad.

Putting down the basket, I hitched a shaky breath and dropped into the seat she'd indicated. The chair's front legs sank and settled on the soft lawn. "I met him at a welcome party organized by the Chinese Student Association at OSU. A bunch of us sat near the entrance. Every time someone strolled in, especially a guy, my girlfriends would make witty comments. When Ken walked in, the woman sitting next to me whispered, 'This guy is very tall.' I looked at him, unimpressed. He had on a pair of thick, myopic glasses."

Mom squinted. "In your first year at OSU, whenever you told me about some man asking you out, you complained their attention annoyed you."

I reached down and plucked a dandelion from the grass, hoping the bright yellow could cheer me. "I distrusted dating and marriage."

I didn't need another heartbreaking experience in my life. Although I emerged from my cocoon, I feared getting betrayed and hurt. "God had a different plan for me."

I slouched deeper into the lawn chair and let memories sweep over me.

On the Sunday following the welcome party, I met Ken at church. My impression of him became even worse because he spoke Mandarin with a strange accent.

He seemed not to care as he introduced himself, saying he grew up in Hong Kong. After graduating from high school, he went to the State University of New York at Buffalo and received a bachelor's degree in civil engineering. He came to Ohio State University for his master's.

Before I said anything, a girl nearby launched into a long conversation with him. I excused myself and left.

In the fall of that year, I spent most of my time in the main library, studying for my PhD candidacy written exam. Whenever I grew tired, I stared through the window at the Oval, the huge open space at the center of our school, with lush, manicured grass and geometric-patterned walkways.

On an atypical warm afternoon, I peeled my gaze away from my textbook, *Principles of Biochemistry*. Many fellow students lay on the lawn, chatting and basking in the sun's warmth. As if enchanted by a magic spell, I ambled outside.

"Hi, Ruth." When someone called my name, I sighted Ken, clad in shorts and a tank top, sitting beneath a tree. He raised a hand. "Please sit down."

I tipped my head toward the blue sky, the weak autumn rays warming my face.

"Please come join me." He patted the grass beside him.

Should I? Or should I not?

Heat crept up to my cheeks as I sat.

He thrust his hands into the pockets of his shorts and leaned his head back against the trunk. "My uncle lives in Taiwan. I've been there. Have you ever been to Hong Kong?"

"No." I focused on a wilted dandelion nearby.

Ken shifted his body closer. "Ah, you ought to go. It's a unique place that weaves Western and Asian cultures together."

Embarrassment tied my tongue. After an awkward silence, I checked my watch and stood up. "I'd better get back to my study."

"Ruth?" Mom's voice pulled me back from my reverie. "When did he ask you out? Right after the welcome party?"

"No, not so soon." I shook my head. Thinking about how I stared at the dead dandelion to avoid looking at Ken at OSU, I twirled the fresh one I'd plucked a few minutes ago. "We got acquainted, but our conversations circled superficial topics. I learned he was the only son in the family. His father was a pastor, and his parents and one sister still lived in Hong Kong. I didn't pay him special attention until a friend talked about him."

Mom cocked her head, her eyes bright as a bird about to pounce on a worm. "Yeah?"

"Maggie from church, with whom I became close, praised him nonstop. It was always Ken this or Ken that from her." I mimicked Maggie's soprano voice. "'Ken is different from other guys. Ken is the one who picks up the garbage at our fellowship meetings. Ken plays the piano for the choir during our Sunday worship. Ken's demeanor is consistently polite, gentle, and patient to everyone.'"

Mom's eyes had grown even brighter. Why was she suddenly so engrossed in our romance? I imagined how the worm must feel wriggling and trying to hide from the eager bird.

As I hesitated about whether to continue, Ken opened the French door and strolled over. "Hi, Mom. Hi, Ruth."

Whew. I'd never been so happy to see him.

Mom hopped from her seat and picked up the basket. "I'd better go in and cook dinner."

After she left, I stood to hug Ken. "Mom was asking me about our OSU days."

"Yes?" He gave my nose a gentle peck, then kissed me on the lips. I shut my eyes to savor the tender moment.

When he released his hold of me, I grasped his hand. "Do you remember Maggie? Have you ever gone out with her?"

He paused and touched his chin. "Such a long time ago. Who can remember? Let's go in. It's getting dark."

Chapter Ten

On Saturday, Mom walked into the kitchen. "Mimi, what're you doing?"

"Just having my daily dose of oatmeal." I looked up from my phone.

She pulled out the chair beside me. "Last night you mentioned you still have the picture of you sitting on your dad's shoulder. Could you show it to me?"

Putting down the spoon, I grabbed my laptop from my study and searched through a file named "Scanned Childhood Mementos." I retrieved the photo to show Mom. "Here you go."

A grin crinkled up her cheeks. "The checkerboard dress looked so cute on you."

"You made it from scratch, right?" How many times had I seen my mother sewing in our family room? Her skillful hands sewed most of my childhood clothes.

Her smile faded. "I wish your dad were still alive. He would be so proud of you. I never dreamed you would get your PhD and become an accomplished scientist."

"Me neither." Taking the laptop back from her, I eyed the laughing little girl. "Back in university, I wasn't a career-minded person. After Ken and I became steady sweethearts, I planned to give up my studies to marry him."

"But God led you down a different path." As if charting a course, Mom traced a finger across the tablecloth.

I set the laptop aside, grabbed my spoon, and dipped it into the bowl. "Do you remember Anne from OSU?"

"Of course." She flattened her palms on the table. "She shared the gospel with me. On the spot, I accepted Christ as my savior. Why do you bring up Anne?"

"She and her husband are coming to Chicago next weekend. We plan to get together." I showed her Anne's text message. "While I was in college, you refused to go to church. When you visited me in Columbus, you agreed to attend worship with me. What made you change your mind?"

Mom scratched her forehead. "Pastor Ning, Anne, and many others were so kind to me. When you were busy in the lab, they showed me around the city. Plus, I finally saw the changes in your behavior." She curved up one corner of her mouth. "I haven't seen Anne since I left Columbus. It would be nice to see her again. Should we eat at home? I can make steamed fish and shrimp scampi."

"Yum. I can't wait." I licked my lips to tease her. "By the way, I found this."

I retrieved a photo from another file on my laptop. Inside stood Mrs. Hu, a widow from our church in Columbus, Anne and her husband, David, and Ken and I.

Mom tilted the laptop as if fighting a glare on the screen. "How young and carefree you and Ken looked. Were you dating by then? Tell me how you two got started."

Oops. I shouldn't have shown her the picture. I edged away, uncertain whether to oblige her. When I was at OSU, she didn't like Ken at all, and I hid our courtship from her. Why did she become interested now?

Mom reached for me and drew me in tight. "I'm curious what falling in love feels like."

Yeah, she never went through the courting process.

Should I share that part of my past with her?

Drawing a deep breath, I searched for my diary on my laptop. Last year, I scanned and digitized all my diaries, except the earlier ones my aunt threw out. With a few clicks, I found what I was looking for.

August 12: Hot summer day. I stayed in my room to pray, asking for wisdom from the Lord.

Recently, I've developed unsettling feelings toward Ken. We aren't compatible at all. He doesn't speak Taiwanese. Mom won't be happy if I'm involved with someone like him. Plus, he plans to return to Hong Kong after he graduates. God has called him to serve as a pastor there. I can never live in Hong Kong. I don't even know a word of Cantonese.

Ken called me after lunch, turning today into one of my most memorable days. The following is a verbatim account of the exchanges between us and the agitated feelings inside of me.

"Do you have time this afternoon? Can you meet me by the east side of Mirror Lake?"

My heart skipped a beat. I forced myself to speak in a calm tone. "What is it about?"

"I have some personal matters to share with you." His voice sounded lower than usual.

I leaned against my bedroom wall, a gust of warmth traveling from my neck to my cheeks. "Can you tell me over the phone?"

"I can't. It has to be in person."

I arrived on time for our meeting. As soon as I approached, he stopped pacing and looked at me with an intense gaze.

I scratched my head in bewilderment. "What's the matter with you?"

The next moment is still a pleasant blur in my mind, like a pink rose in a fog or a gorgeous view from a distance.

He declared his special attachment to me.

We talked about how we felt and what we were afraid of.

The guidance of the Holy Spirit overwhelmed me. "This morning, I prayed about us."

Ken chuckled. "We shouldn't deny our feelings. Let's go a step further and see how God leads us."

On my way back to the dorm, I was floating, not walking.

My life has taken a different direction.

I scanned through my diary, then handed it over to show Mom

the entry.

She began, then paused. "So, you thought I wouldn't be happy if you dated him?"

When I nodded, she proceeded to read. "Such a coincidence. You're right to say the Holy Spirit guided you two." She gave the laptop back to me. "It's a factual account, devoid of emotions except for a few sentences. Is that all there is to it? Falling in love seems overrated."

No, there was a lot more. I checked the entries in August again and paused on one page dated two weeks later.

> August 26: The taste of love turns out to be sweeter than I've ever imagined.
>
> Something must be happening. My body feels lighter than usual as if I'm airborne. The air smells fragrant, and the grass of the Oval looks extraordinarily green. I smile for no reason while working in the lab. Even my lab mates wonder what has happened to me.
>
> I want to see Ken as much as possible. But he's more rational and says that, since we're both busy with our studies, we should only meet every other day and pray together once a week.
>
> I came up with a lame excuse. "If we study together in the library, does it count as a date?"
>
> He laughed and said we have to sit in different sections.
>
> Time crawls on the days I don't see him. It doesn't help that I constantly glance at the clock. I've never had such an intense longing for someone before. Is this what falling in love feels like?

Well, what could it harm? I gave Mom my laptop again.

She fixed her gaze on the screen. "Ha, now that's more like it."

I fidgeted as she perused my innermost emotions. Yet she read without remarks until the end. "So, Ken told you he wanted to be a pastor early on. As much as I know him, he would be straightforward from the beginning."

Mom knew Ken's character so well. "He discussed it with me soon after we started dating."

I searched the diary for another entry. An image of a young and love-struck me emerged. I must have placed particular importance on that interaction. Otherwise, why would I write another verbatim account of the conversation between Ken and me?

September 20: In the morning, while strolling around Mirror Lake, Ken talked to me about the future. "When I was a sophomore at SUNY Buffalo, I felt God calling me to serve Him full time as a pastor. Originally, I attempted to enter a seminary to study theology after college. But my parents didn't approve of my decision. My dad suggested I gained a few years of working experience. That's why I'm here at OSU." He paused and looked at me. "I think God is still calling me. Will it bother you if I don't work as a civil engineer in the future?"

He shared his dream with me. I clutched a fist to my chest. "You'll be an excellent pastor."

He exhaled a deep relief.

I gestured for us to sit on a patch of grass along the walking path. "I told Anne we're dating. Hope you don't mind."

"You did?" His eyes opened wide. "What did she say?"

I bent over to pluck up a dandelion. "She got so excited for us that she gave me a booklet. It touches on some critical issues that young people seldom talk about during courtship."

"What issues?" He edged closer.

Sensing him so close, I detected a trace of embarrassment in my heart. "Life goals, friendships, money, and other important topics. She suggested we go over it together. She said it'll help us build our relationship on a solid foundation with God in the center." Filled with unease, I pulled apart the yellow petals. "Should we start reading it next week?"

"Of course. Anne is so kind." Ken flashed a tentative smile, then rubbed his forehead. "I also told Mrs. Hu about us."

"Yeah?" I dropped the weed.

Ken picked up the broken-up flower and examined it in his palm. "As you know, she's a straight talker. She challenged me right away about whether I still plan to return home after my graduation. I said yes, and She lectured me for ten long minutes. She doesn't think you'll be happy living in Hong

Kong. She reminded me you don't speak a word of Cantonese."

At once, the suppressed fear deep inside rushed to the surface. I blurted out, "Can you serve the Lord as a pastor in the US?"

Ken shook his head. "The year 1997 is coming up soon. Britain plans to give Hong Kong back to China. Some suspect China will liberate Hong Kong right away, but nobody can predict the future. I want to be a pastor to help my fellow Christians face the uncertainties." Agitation crept into his eyes. "Although I liked you from the beginning, I hesitated to ask you out because of this."

Heat blurred my vision. "What made you overcome your hesitation?"

He dipped his chin. "I prayed about it for a long time and received the words from the Lord, 'Don't fear. Trust and obey, and leave the outcome to me.' So, I mustered up my courage to call you on that Saturday."

After Mom finished reading, she placed my laptop on the table. "Did you know about 1997 before that conversation?"

"No. I only knew he intended to return to Hong Kong after his graduation." I shook my head. "Once he brought it up, anxiety seized me. But it was too late. I was hopelessly in love and would do anything to be with him."

"Despite not speaking a word of Cantonese, you went to Hong Kong with him. People say love is the most powerful force in this world. Now I'm convinced." Mom grasped my hand. "Brothers and sisters in Columbus were so loving toward us. I can't wait to see Anne and David again next weekend. Too bad Mrs. Hu passed away already."

"Yeah." I played with her fingers. "Anne told me a few years ago."

Mom dragged in a short breath. "Aging and death. That's life."

"Oh, don't say that." I hugged her shoulders.

"No problem. We learn to accept it." She held me at arm's length, then said in a more cheerful tone, "What's your plan for today?"

Beyond the French door, the glowing July sunshine filtered through tree branches, casting odd-shaped shadows on the patio.

"Nice weather. Do you want to go to the botanic garden? Roses are still in bloom."

"Good idea. I love roses." Her face brightened. "Don't you have to take Jonny to his piano lesson and martial arts exercise?"

"No worries. I'll ask Ken to help."

***

As we entered the Chicago Botanic Garden in Glencoe, I directed Mom's attention to some equipment. "This place is famous for its vast ground and millions of plants in a variety of settings. Should we get an electric conveyance vehicle?"

Her nose scrunched with her puckered pout. "An ECV? Am I that old?"

Snickering, I patted her arm. "It'll give us the option, should you or I become tired."

"Good idea." She stepped on an ECV and figured out how to maneuver it.

"You're so smart." I jostled her shoulder. "No wonder you could manage the Japanese immigration system to become a citizen."

I wanted to add, "Why can't you control your weight and eating habit? They'll help you improve your health." But I bit my lip, afraid of spoiling the wonderful day.

When she sped up toward the rose garden, I quickened my steps, barely able to catch up.

"Wow, yellow roses, my favorite." She paused by a patch of cheery flowers.

A pleasant scent wafted in the air. I sucked in a deep breath and took a picture of Mom. "Does one of your church friends in Tokyo grow roses? You've got to show her this photo."

"Yes, Heidi. She and her husband, Dennis, are kind to me." She stood up from the ECV and dipped her face to a large rose, closing her eyes as she breathed in. "They always ask me about you. Heidi keeps saying it's tough to be a pastor's wife and how she admires you. She wonders how you handle the congregation's scrutiny."

I trailed after her. "I met them when I visited you last time. Isn't Dennis a nephrologist? He showed a great deal of interest in my research."

"Yes." She squinted up at me, the sun in her face. "We've never talked about this. Is it difficult to be a pastor's wife? What's your

70

biggest challenge?"

Caught by surprise, I averted my gaze toward the blue sky. "I paid for Ken's studies at the seminary. All along, I thought I was ready to be a pastor's wife." I rubbed a sudden chill from my arms. "Yet at our first church, I struggled. I tried to fulfill the expectations of others but felt miserable."

One corner of Mom's mouth crinkled up. "Ah, that's when you came to Japan by yourself. We took a trip to Hokkaidō together. Did it help? How did you get over the initial shock?"

I grasped her hand and helped her get back on the ECV. "It took me a while to figure out that I only needed to please my Lord, not others. My gift is teaching. I'm good at grabbing the audience's attention and can use different ways to convey a message."

Two hours later, we entered a woody area.

"What's that?" Mom pointed at a plaque in front of a gorgeous Japanese maple.

I went over to study it. An inscription said, "In memory of our beloved mother..."

"The botanic garden has a program for people to dedicate a tree in memory of a loved one. They'll place a personalized tag by the tree for its whole life."

She gaped at the maple. "Don't do that for me. After I die, cremate my body and scatter the ashes into the Pacific Ocean if you can. If it's too much trouble, just do it in your backyard."

A chill crept up into my heart. "Why do you say that on such a beautiful day?"

The nightmares in the years following Dad's death came rushing back. I jammed both hands into my armpits, clamping down on my fear of losing Mom.

"Why not? How come you sounded so fearful?" She tilted her face up toward the sky, the expression of perfect peace as she basked in the sun's glow filtered through that maple. "It's okay to talk about death. We all have to go that way sooner or later. No, I have no fear."

Pent-up words rolled off my tongue. "If you lose some weight and watch your diet, you'll live to a hundred."

She glared at me. "What's the point of living to a hundred? The quality of life is more important than its length."

I turned away to control my emotions. I was not ready to talk about this subject. "Let's go. I asked Ken to cook spaghetti and meat sauce for us."

Yet dread refused to lift. I feigned calmness, then gestured her ahead of me. "Come on. Lunch is probably waiting for us already."

Chapter Eleven

On the next Saturday, a sedan pulled into our driveway, and Anne's tall figure came into view. I rushed over. "Anne."

She hugged me, a broad smile curving up her cheeks. Seeing my mother, she shifted over. "Auntie, I haven't seen you since you left Columbus some twenty years ago. You look good."

Ken shook hands with David. "You've not changed much, except more tanned. Did you just come back from your Puerto Rico short-term mission trip?"

Our neighbor walked by and gave us curious glances. I drew Anne to the side. "We'd better get inside. My mom still has to steam the fish. She wants to make sure it's hot and fresh for you and David."

In the kitchen, a delightful aroma swirled around us.

Anne gave Mom a thumbs-up. "Auntie, you're a superb cook." Then she looped her arm through mine. "Where's your son?"

"He went to my aunt's house to have a sleepover with his cousin," Ken answered for me. "How are your daughters? Are they working?"

"Yes. Finally, both found jobs they liked. Praise the Lord." David touched his fingertips together.

While he talked about where their daughters worked, Anne patted Mom's hand. "How is your health?"

Mom frowned. "Not too well. I have diabetes."

"Oh no." Anne's eyes opened wide. "Is it serious? When did it start?"

"In my mid-forties, I became thirsty all the time and had to go to the bathroom frequently. I thought little of the signs until I began to feel weak and exhausted every day." Mom furrowed her brows tighter. "When I went to the doctor, my blood sugar reached a sky-high level."

My mouth fell open, and my mind spiraled down a dark hole. She never told me about that. What else was she hiding?

As the irrational fear of losing my mother seized me, my muscles tensed up.

Anne hugged Mom's shoulders tight. "My father suffers from diabetes too. It's a tough disease to manage."

"Yeah, it's a multifactorial disease." I forced calmness into my voice and shifted my gaze to Anne. "How about you? Do you have any health issues?"

"Luckily, no." She scratched her forehead.

Mom chimed in. "Aren't you a few years older than Mimi? She has high cholesterol. How do you keep your body in such amazing shape?"

Anne's lips curled up into a smile. "I control my weight and watch my diet. Plus, a few years ago, I ran into a doctor who taught me to massage my feet."

"See?" I gave Mom a meaningful look. "Two simple steps can do a lot."

She glared back.

I didn't dare go further and lowered my chin to subdue my emotions. "How interesting. I also met a doctor who said foot massage can help improve health."

On one of our visits to Ken's family in Hong Kong—back when China had just opened to tourists—we joined a tour to Shanghai. One of my teeth gave me trouble. The pain became quite intolerable. Then, Ken directed my attention toward an advertisement that a doctor specializing in reflexology resided within our hotel.

As I described my experience, Anne flicked both eyebrows up. "Aha, was the name of your hotel the Purple Mountain Place?"

I gasped. "How did you know?"

"We must have encountered the same doctor." Anne braced a hand on the quartz counter and raised the other. "What a coincidence."

Mom crossed her arms over her chest, her head cocked to one side. "Now you have me intrigued. Tell me what happened."

I couldn't help grinning, and my shoulders relaxed. "I decided to give it a try. A large, middle-aged woman greeted me at the office. Feeling rather foolish, I spoke in Mandarin and said I had a toothache. She wiped my right foot thoroughly with alcohol, then pressed along the length of my sole. Pausing at one spot, she raised her head. 'You had bronchitis recently?'"

Mom wrinkled her nose. "Did you?"

"Must be the same doctor," Anne blurted out. "She massaged my feet and informed me, 'You have a diabetic family background.'"

"Extraordinary!" Mom's eyes grew wide. "She could tell from examining your feet?"

"I had the same interaction with her." I bopped my head. "She went ahead and showed me the place I need to work on to delay the onset of diabetes."

A fruit fly circled in, and Mom fanned it away. "What happened to your toothache?"

"She pressed hard on one of my toes. It hurt like crazy, but my toothache subsided."

"Unbelievable." Mom brought a hand to her freshly dyed hair.

"Yeah." I smiled again. "She said the pain would return and taught me how to massage that toe. I completed the trip without a hitch. Being trained in the Western scientific tradition, I used to object to anything related to Chinese medicine and alternative healing. The trip to Shanghai changed my perspective."

"Are you talking about the doctor in Shanghai?" Ken must have overheard our conversation. "Ruth came back to our hotel room in bewilderment. I went to see the doctor even though I didn't have any health issues."

"Hey, how did you figure out what we were discussing in Taiwanese?" I chuckled and switched to Mandarin. "Thirty minutes later, Ken came back with a puzzled expression and said, 'She studied my feet and stated I'd had appendicitis previously. She asked me why I wanted to see her since my health is excellent.'"

"Such a fond anecdote." Anne laughed as we brought food over to the table. "Ken, how're your parents doing? I met them once when Dave and I visited Hong Kong. Is your father still serving at the same Methodist church where you grew up?"

"Yes."

After saying grace, Ken placed a piece of sea bass onto Mom's plate.

Anne's eyes twinkled. "Have you learned to speak Taiwanese?"

He flashed a sheepish grin. "I picked up a few words here and there, but it doesn't seem to matter anymore."

"I'm glad things turned out well for you two." Anne grasped my hand. "I still remember the day you came to my OSU office in tears."

David lifted his chin. "Why? What was it about? You've never mentioned it."

Anne glanced at me as if asking whether she should spill my secrets. I placed a finger to my lips, then took a bite of the fish on my plate. "Wow, so tender."

"Yeah, it's excellent." Anne nodded. "Dave, I'll tell you later. Ken, how is your sister doing? Is she still teaching pipe organ?"

I lost track of the conversation. Ann's words brought to my mind a segment of my past full of God's mercy amid dread and misery. I seldom revisited that part of my life, for it roused such edginess in me.

After Ken and I went steady, I called my mom to tell her.

She responded in a terse tone. "Is he the tall fellow from Hong Kong who didn't understand a word I uttered when I visited Columbus?"

My agitation grew stronger. "Is that your only dislike of him?"

"Didn't you tell me he planned to return to Hong Kong after graduation? Will you go with him? You won't be happy there. You don't even speak Cantonese. How can you survive?"

The exuberant feeling of falling in love vanished without a trace after our call. When I told Ken, I learned his parents also disapproved of our relationship. I gawked at him. "Why? Is it the same reason?"

He placed a palm on his forehead. "My dad reminded me that if I plan to serve in Hong Kong as a pastor, I should date someone from Hong Kong."

"What a practical suggestion." I couldn't hide my sarcasm. "You once told me your dad never spoke a harsh word to you or anybody else, and you always appreciate his advice. I suppose you'll listen to him?"

"Ruth." Ken reached for a Kleenex to wipe away the sweat. "I believe God is working between us. Please don't lose heart. Let's wait for the Lord to lead us."

A fruit fly flew in front of me, interrupting my train of thought.

David's loud voice sounded. "What a pest. They're everywhere. We have them at home too." He shooed another fly away. "We helped organize Vacation Bible School programs for local kids in San Juan. Using themed activities, we taught children to love Jesus. It's an outstanding way to reach out to non-Christian family members."

I straightened my spine. When did the conversation turn to their Puerto Rico mission trip?

Ken's chopstick paused. "Do you speak Spanish?"

"No, we don't. Luckily, most of the people speak English." David leaned back against the chair. "Maybe the mission work helps us more than..."

While the men launched into a long discussion about why outreach improved the health of a church, Anne's cell rang. She walked to the corner to answer the phone, then returned to her husband. "Dave, we'd better go. My sister is waiting for us to go shopping together."

After the guests left and Ken returned to his study to work on his Sunday sermon, Mom stood to collect the empty plates. "Nice to see Anne again. She's so kind."

I scraped the leftovers together. "Yeah. She and David love the Lord very much. They eagerly share that love with others."

As if thinking of something important, she lifted a stack of dishes and cocked her head at me. "Anne mentioned you went to see her at her OSU office—crying. What was it about?"

"Oh, that." I dipped my chin. "You won't be interested."

"Of course, I'm interested. Tell me." Her searching look cowed me. "It must have something to do with you and Ken, right?"

Not hearing a response from me, she clattered utensils onto the dirty dishes. "I had health issues, and you asked me not to attend your graduation ceremony. In our weekly phone conversations, you never mentioned anything unusual, except that you planned to move to Northwestern University in Chicago. The next thing I knew, you were in Hong Kong preparing for your wedding. What happened during those months?"

"How could I tell you about my plan? You didn't approve of Ken." I plopped back into my chair, a jittery heat surging through me.

She came to sit by me. "I'm sorry. I disliked Ken without even trying to know him."

I rubbed my now-throbbing temples. "We fought every time I mentioned Ken. You disappointed me, and I thought you would never change your opinion."

"I love you very much. I always have your best interest at heart."

"You say that all the time!" The words burst out with the heat boiling over. "Sometimes, it feels like a guilt trip."

Ouch. I cringed. Had I said *that* aloud?

"I didn't mean to cause you pain." Mom tilted her head up. "How about the job at Northwestern University?"

I accepted the subject change. "My PhD advisor did make an excellent arrangement for me. One of his friends at Northwestern read my four papers. Dr. Phillips told him I had a pair of amazing hands. Whatever experiments I touched on always yielded wonderful results. The professor was impressed that I entered the PhD program as a college graduate and received my doctorate in three years and nine months. He offered me a position in his lab."

Her eyes stretched wide. "And you turned it down?"

"Yes." I blinked to refocus. "Ken urged me to come to Hong Kong and insisted his salary as an engineer could sustain us as a family. I agreed. Since I held a Taiwanese passport, I needed to obtain a visa first. Because I wrote down marriage, not tourism, for my reason to visit, the British embassy office informed me it would take some time before they could give me a decision, perhaps three months or more. I didn't want to start a new job without knowing what would happen next."

A frown tightened her lips. "Didn't OSU terminate your dorm lease?"

"They did." I inclined my head. "Mrs. Hu invited me to move into the spare room in her house."

Mom heaved an audible breath. "Mrs. Hu looked out for young people. Too bad she's no longer with us."

"Although she treated me well, she tried hard to persuade me not to go to Hong Kong."

I could still hear her now.... "Pardon my language. You're foolish to give up your biochemistry career in the US and go to Hong Kong. You have a PhD, and Ken only has a master's. You'll find a guy better than him."

"Don't you think she gave you sound and practical advice?" Mom interrupted my memories. "If I'd known, I would have spoken the same words."

"Precisely why I didn't tell you about my plan." I brought a palm to my chest, hoping to vanquish my emotions. "Her words affected my resolve. I reasoned with God, 'Lord, with my F-1 student visa, after graduation, I can only stay in the US legally without a job for a while. I can't keep waiting.' Yet whenever I prayed about it, the Lord gave me a Bible verse."

She drew her chair closer. "What does it say?"

I clicked my cell phone to show her Psalm 111:2 as I repeated the quote. "'Great are the works of the Lord; they are pondered by all who delight in them.'"

"Did you interpret it as a promise from God?"

I rested an elbow on the table and leaned my head on my hand. "The Bible verse brought me solace, but the uncertainties drained me both physically and emotionally. Last year, when I scanned my diaries into digital files, I noticed I raised a question several times, 'Lord, I don't speak a word of Cantonese. If Ken attends the seminary, can I find a job to support him?'"

"It must have been difficult for you." Her eyes glowed, the tender concern in them softening my heart.

"Worse, one afternoon, I received an envelope with unfamiliar handwriting on it. I tore it open. Ken's mother wrote the letter. She described how my relationship with her son had torn the family apart and begged me not to write to him again." As the painful memory intruded, I blinked to prevent tears.

"Oh, Mimi." Mom pulled me to her bosom.

"I'm fine." Easing away, I forced a smile. "I turned to God once more, and He replied with the same words, 'Great are the works of the Lord.' At last, I surrendered to God and said a silent prayer. 'Lord, I'll wait until I get an answer from the British embassy. If they give me the visa, I'll go.'"

Mom patted my arm. "I suppose you received your visa in time to travel to Hong Kong?"

"Before the end of three months, I secured my visa." I fiddled with my sleeve to calm down. "Upon my arrival, Ken took me to an elderly lady's house and introduced us. Auntie Audrey watched him grow up in their church and welcomed me to stay at her house."

"How did Ken's parents change their minds?"

"God did great works." Warmth crept into my heart. "The next morning, a few more women came to see me. Auntie Audrey said they'd all known Ken since he was a baby. They took me shopping and treated me to lunch. One of them handed me a book with some cassette tapes: *Cantonese for Mandarin Speakers*."

"You learned Cantonese that way?" Her eyes opened wide. "Those aunties must have intervened."

"Through them, God fulfilled His promise to me." I pressed my palms to the tablecloth, thinking of the home and family we had built—the gift from God. "Three weeks later, Ken told me his mother had picked a day for our wedding. He said a few people talked to his parents and persuaded them we were well suited for each other."

Mom gave me a teasing wink. "You informed me only after you and Ken had planned everything."

"Even then, you sounded reluctant to travel to Hong Kong."

"Didn't I give you my blessings and attend your wedding?" Her lips crinkled up into a grin. "Our lives are full of God's mercy and grace. If you didn't get the visa, most likely you and Ken wouldn't be together."

Apparently, the British government in Hong Kong had sent Ken a letter requesting an interview with him. They wanted to make sure it wasn't a sham marriage before giving me the visa. "You're right. Someday, I'm going to write a book in which the heroine didn't get her visa to Hong Kong."

An unrelated thought entered my mind. Mom seemed interested in the story about the reflexology doctor. "Massaging feet may help improve your diabetes. Do you want to give it a try? I bought a lot of foot massage tools and can give you one."

She put a hand to her mouth and yawned. "Cooking and talking with guests exhausted me. I need a nap."

Right. I stifled the urge to grind my teeth. "Go. I'll take care of the cleanup."

Alone in the kitchen, I stood to pick up the plates, then sat again. Did seeing old friends always trigger such intense emotions?

I shook my head. Still, my mind refused to drop the thought of those days full of grief, joy, and occasional anger, especially the immediate few months after Ken graduated and went back to Hong Kong as planned.

On his day of departure, a few of us, including Anne, saw him off at the airport. He placed a cassette tape into my palm before boarding. In it, he declared his love toward me and emphasized that, with the Lord's mercy, we could sustain our relationship even separated by the Pacific Ocean.

Yet for months, I wept every day. We called once a week but often ended up arguing about the future. I had little faith and thought we would go different ways, although the mere idea of leaving Ken for good pierced my heart like a dagger.

In my daily prayers, I'd repeatedly asked God what would become of us.

"Ruth, come here."

Ken's urgent call drew me back to the present. I strolled into his office. "What's up? Are you done with your sermon?"

A pile of letters caught my eye.

"Not yet." He grinned. "I want to show you this."

"Aren't those the letters we wrote to each other during our separation?"

"Yes, but that's not why I called you." He pulled me to sit on his lap and showed me a magnet. "Look at this memento."

I studied the words—*Let the wild thunder roar; together we are safe.*

"Our old friends' visit brought back many recollections, some painful, some sweet. I'm not sure what this one belongs to."

"It's both." I turned to kiss him. "Tears mingled with laughter."

His eyes sparkled. "Do you remember that Saturday? I borrowed my roommate's car to take you to a park not far from campus. We intended to seek God's guidance for our future amid nature. Halfway down a country road, a thunderstorm broke out, and we had a flat tire."

Fragments of a scene crossed my mind.

While large raindrops fell, we walked to the nearby gas station to seek help. Ken held his umbrella over me, although his whole body got soaked. Right there, I told myself I'd never find another person like him.

I tapped his chin. "Of course, I remember. Amid the rain, I cemented my commitment to you."

"What a coincidence." He gave my nose a gentle peck. "That night, I prayed a lot and made up my mind. I wouldn't marry anyone else but you. The next morning, I went to the bookstore and found this for you."

"Yeah. You handed me the gift bag and said, 'As long as the Lord is with us, we'll be all right.'"

I examined the inscription again. "I'm thankful for our journey together. All the twists and turns make it interesting. I believe risks and challenges are important ingredients of the abundant life the Lord has promised us."

"Sure thing." Ken released his hold on me. "Talking about challenges, I'd better finish my sermon for tomorrow. Let's talk later tonight."

Chapter Twelve

"Last week when I played Monopoly with Jonny, he said he's always so busy and has little time to play games." Mom stood up from harvesting chives and wrapped her well-worn shirt tighter around her, even though the early August evening held pleasant warmth.

I wrinkled my nose, breathing in the tangy chive scent. "How did you understand him? Maybe you misunderstood what he meant."

She separated the chives into six plastic bags. "Why are you so blind? Everybody can see the child is overloaded. During school days, he has piano and art lessons. On top of that, he goes to martial arts and Chinese language classes. Once the summer vacation started, you sent him to different camps every week, and he still has to go to all the activities."

She had no idea what it was like to raise an active American boy. I tapped my foot. "It's important to keep him busy. Many children get into trouble because they have too much free time. Plus, extracurricular programs give him the chance to explore his interests and teach him to be responsible."

"I'm not saying those things are bad." She bumped my shoulder with hers. "I should say you and Ken have done a great job with Jonny. He's such a sweet, kindhearted boy. Still, children are children. There's only one childhood. Let him enjoy being a kid."

Being a kid... Living in a small village, I roamed the countryside every day after school with my friends. We walked every trail, swam every stream, and climbed every rock, always as a group. I only felt unhappy when my mother caught me doing something naughty. She would take out the bundled thin bamboo branches from the top of the closet and give me a whack.

I made a silly face with rolling eyes to tease Mom. "Remember you used to spank me? At least we've never punished Jonny with bamboo sticks."

"Times have changed. Back then, discipline always involved spanking, no doubt about it."

Time to change the subject. "Nice to have such an endless supply of chives. Six bags, huh? This time, whom shall we give them to? Maybe the Trinity seminary students? They love to make dumplings and always complain chives are too expensive."

Mom grasped my right hand, and I shrieked with pain. "Ouch."

"What is it?" She straightened her shoulders. "Are you okay?"

I checked the area below my ring finger. It appeared swollen.

Did I bump into something?

"It hurts." I drew my brows together.

Mom smoothed her finger over the spot. "Is it arthritis? You'd better call Dr. Stone."

"Not again. I've already seen her so many times this year." My mouth went dry, and I sucked in my cheeks hard.

I waited for ten more days before calling my doctor. By then, the bump grew so big that I could no longer close my hand to make a fist.

Back in Dr. Stone's office, I scowled at my hand, wondering what went wrong with my health. She examined the swelling. "I'll send you to an orthopedic surgeon right away."

I went to see Dr. Shapiro during the same week. After checking the X-ray pictures, he pivoted his roller chair my way. "Looks like a badly inflamed tendon."

That didn't make sense. I scratched my forehead. "I haven't had any accidents or injuries."

"Repetitive motions can also cause it." He surveyed the films again. "You have a few choices, physical therapy, medications, cortisone shots, or surgery."

I opted for the first.

Three weeks later, my condition got so severe that even picking up a teacup challenged me. My physical therapist gave up. "It's not working. My honest assessment is that you need more aggressive treatment."

Back to square one.

Sitting in Dr. Shapiro's office, I covered my swollen palm with my good hand. "What's going on with me?"

Dr. Shapiro bobbed his head. "I'll give you an injection today. Be prepared. It'll be the worst shot you've ever had in your life. Afterward, the inflammation will subside."

He numbed the area before sticking the needle into the gap between my fingers. I gritted my teeth. Excruciating pain shot through my hand and up every nerve ending in my shoulder.

Forty minutes later, when I stepped down into our living room, a delightful aroma of grilled beef greeted me. Yet I shook my head hard and grimaced at the throbbing ache.

Seeing me, Mom hurried to my side. "You don't look good."

"Even with the doctor's warning, I still found it horrible." I plopped down on the sofa and raised my right hand, which looked like a boxing glove.

She sat by me and pulled me into her bosom. "Poor thing."

I remained quiet, savoring the tender moment and the security of having my mother so close. My mind conjured up an earlier image of Mom with me. Was I four or five? The wind went damp with drizzle. She carried me in her arms. Along the roadside, her feet slid out from under her. Instead of dropping me, she managed to have me land on her lap. After that accident, from time to time, she complained her back hurt.

Mom's fingers brushed across my hair. "Do you want to eat or drink something?"

"I'm fine. Don't go." I played with a button on her shirt. "What am I going to do without you? I can't even hold up a cup. Luckily, I can still handle my laptop. It's so nice of you to cook every meal for us."

"That's what a mother is for." She chuckled.

"Why do you love me so much, even though I often make you angry?"

She patted my cheek. "Such a foolish question. You're my daughter."

"Have you ever wished that you'd never had me?"

"No."

At her immediate response, I wiggled into her embrace as if I was still six years old. "After Dad passed away and before I went to college, how did you keep us fed?"

"I thought you knew."

"We've never talked about that."

Mom raised her gaze toward the ceiling. "Not easy. I don't speak Mandarin. The only job available for someone like me was as a dishwasher in a restaurant. But the fringe benefits were that I got free leftover food all the time."

"I didn't know you were a dishwasher. I thought you were their chef." As my mind turned to those tough days, sorrow mingled with a trace of gentleness, and I snuggled closer, wishing I could somehow care for her as well as she'd cared for me. "We sometimes had rare delicacies, like prawns or even crabs."

"I quit after you graduated from high school." She hitched a breath. "In college, you isolated yourself and never dated."

I cleared my throat, trying to calm the tightness gripping it. "After Dad died, I didn't want to establish a relationship with anyone. I feared losing them and didn't dare take any risks. I figured if I loved no one, it wouldn't hurt when they left me."

"Your dad's passing was too sudden, totally unexpected." Mom sighed again. "Yet the sufferings in the past teach me to appreciate today's blessings from the Lord even more."

"You always handle a dire circumstance better than I do." I used my left hand to pick at a loose thread on her blouse. "Why do you insist on maintaining your apartment in Tokyo? How do you spend your time?"

"Well, language is my main concern. Here I can't go out by myself. In Tokyo, church, friends, and the activities in my senior center keep me busy and happy." She squinted her eyes. "Did I tell you about your auntie Su-Hua? I have lunch with her at least once a week."

I sat up from her arms, my anxiety giving way to annoyance. "Why do you meet with her so frequently? What good can it bring you? I would think twice before meeting with her."

Mom dipped her head, and her voice came out so soft I bent in closer to listen. "Her Japanese is rather limited. Whenever she feels lonely, she calls and asks me out."

My jaw dropped. "How does she communicate with her husband? Does he speak Taiwanese?"

"I raised the same questions. I guess she and her husband, two lone travelers in Paris, got together out of convenience. No, she isn't content with this marriage, either. But they have a boy. She stays with him because of her son."

"You didn't say she has a son."

"I meant to tell you. Somehow, I forgot. Her son is a senior in high school. He'll enter college this fall." She patted her forehead. "I'm growing old. My mind isn't sharp anymore."

"Don't say that." I leaned back against Mom's chest. "What she did to us no longer bothers you? You've let go of her past transgression completely?"

"I don't want to be a hostage to anyone. If I hold my grudge, I'll remain a slave to the person who hurt me." She wrapped an arm around my waist. "Even though you told me you've also forgiven her, somehow I sense you still harbor a deep resentment."

I searched my heart for negative sentiments and couldn't answer Mom.

"Remember you gave me the Chinese translation of *The Hiding Place* and *Night*?" She drummed her fingers on my shoulder.

"What about them?" I sat up so I could see her. My curiosity piqued. "Why did you bring them up?"

"Reading the two books back-to-back helped me learn a precious insight. Both endured horrid persecutions and cruelties under the Nazis. One's experience of horror made him doubt whether an all-powerful, loving God exists. But the other, Corrie ten Boom, a Christian, emerged from the ordeal with her faith strengthened." Mom stopped her hand's movement, and a faraway look glazed her eyes.

"You're frowning." I traced my left-hand index finger over her eyebrows.

She batted my hand away. "What's the difference between them? The author of *Night* felt God didn't understand our sufferings and wouldn't care at all. In Corrie's darkest moment, she realized Christ understood her sufferings because He had gone through all sorts of tortures in the human world, including crucifixion. And even on the cross, Jesus forgave those who crucified Him. Determined to follow the Lord, Corrie later forgave a German guard who abused her in the concentration camp. If she could do it, there's no reason I can't."

Mom was so perceptive. I gaped at her. "If you were given the same opportunities I had, I wonder what accomplishments you would have achieved. Have you ever regretted that you didn't have the chance to pursue your dream?"

A wry smile thinned out her lips. "Before becoming a Christian, I considered it my fate. After I accepted Christ as my Savior, I sense God loves me as much as He loves famous, successful people. Sometimes, being ordinary is a blessing."

Another simple statement. Yet it touched a chord in me. Why was I never satisfied and always fixing my eyes on another mountaintop?

"My company canceled my project and moved my team into a different department. I believe they made a huge mistake. Chronic kidney disease is a tough problem. The drug we were developing has the potential to help a lot of patients...."

No, I couldn't tell her how my new boss bullied me and demanded I include his name in every one of my scientific papers.

I swallowed hard and mustered up my courage. "What do you think if I resign and set up a biotech start-up?"

She sucked in a shaky breath. "Are you aware of the Chinese saying, 'If you hate someone, convince him to start a business?' It's so risky to be your own boss. Although I know nothing about biotech, I'm aware of friends who filed for bankruptcy after their plans failed."

I rubbed my temple and pinched my lips together.

She stroked her throat. "Have you prayed about it? Have you discussed it with Ken? What did he say?"

"I—"

Ken and Jonny walked into the living room.

"Mommy, Nana." Jonny rushed over and piled on top of me and Mom, his giggles lilting through the air.

"Watch out." Mom raised my right hand to avoid it being hit. "Your mommy got a shot in her palm earlier this afternoon."

Jonny stood up, his dear face crumpling. "Mommy, are you better?"

I nodded. He leaned on me and grasped my left arm. After giving me a tender kiss, he pointed toward a spot on my elbow. "What's this?"

I straightened up from Mom and examined the area. A swelling was visible. When I touched it, it hurt a little.

Did I bump into another hard object? Unlikely.

A distinct chill crept into my heart.

My expression must have worried Mom and Jonny. In unison, they asked if I was okay, their high-pitched voices and different languages blending.

I summoned a shaky smile. "I'm fine. I do need to call my doctor, though."

Chapter Thirteen

The next day, bracing my elbows on my office desk, I listened to the voice message on the company phone. "This is Dr. Nelson. We met last year at the nephrology workshop. I saw your recent paper..."

Yes, I remembered him, a professor at the University of Pittsburgh. He asked if I would be interested in giving a seminar in his department in the fall.

I examined my right palm and left elbow. Should I accept his invitation? Would I be able to handle it?

My cell phone rang, and Ken's contact flashed across the screen. "Hello?"

"My aunt would like to have dinner with us. Since Mom's arrival, they've been wanting to get together with her. Will Mom go this time?"

I rubbed my furrowed brows. "I don't think so. She found it awkward. They don't speak Taiwanese, and she can't understand them."

"Okay. I'll tell my aunt. Ruthy? You sound preoccupied. What's the matter?"

Warmth flooded my heart. My husband knew me. "Someone invited me to give a talk in the fall. I'm deciding whether to accept it or not."

"Are you worried about your physical condition? When will you see Dr. Stone again?"

"Thursday." I stood, then plopped back down in the chair, agitation stirring up. "I'm supposed to be in the prime of my career, but I have a hunch my life is heading into a precarious tunnel."

He kept silent. Then his tone, gentler than usual, rose. "You stepped into biochemistry by chance. After you received your PhD, you were ready to obey God's guidance and give it up. But just like God gave Isaac back to Abraham, He didn't take biochemistry away from you."

I had to agree. I went to Hong Kong, prepared to become a stay-at-home wife and mother. After we were married, an ad in the *South China Morning Post* caught my attention. A certain professor at the Chinese University of Hong Kong had an opening for a research fellow to study membrane proteins.

"Yeah, Dr. James MacKay."

Dr. MacKay, a Scot and a visiting professor from the University of Cambridge, received a grant from the Cancer Research Campaign, UK. He provided me a chance with his research program even though I had no experience in that field.

Ken chuckled. "You did great there. How many papers did you publish out of that project?"

"Seven or eight. I lost count." My mouth curled up. Still, I had to tease my husband. "Now, my dear Pastor Ken, please explain why God wanted Abraham to sacrifice Isaac as an offering. Didn't He instruct the Israelites in Deuteronomy not to do so?"

"Humph." He sounded thoughtful. I could almost see the feigned annoyance on his face together with his laughing eyes. "Such a tough question."

"Well?" I pressed. "We've never discussed that. I'm curious how you interpret it."

He huffed. "By the time Isaac became a young lad, Abraham loved him so much that he had usurped God's position to become his father's idol. As a young person, being someone's god was an unbearable burden, which did more harm than good for both Isaac and Abraham. God had to deal with the issue."

I smiled. Abraham didn't fail the challenge. The ram mentioned later in the story symbolized Christ, the sacrificial lamb from God, that died on the cross for us. "God used an extraordinary way to solve the problem."

A rustling sound accompanied Ken's chuckle. "Feeling better? If not, think about the fringe benefits while you worked for Dr. MacKay. All those eels for breakfast, lunch, and dinner."

What was he doing with that noise? "How can I forget?"

Those enormous sea creatures slithered through my mind. We collected red blood cells from them to study nucleoside transporters on their cell membranes. Before that, I didn't know red blood cells from an eel, unlike those from mammals, have a cell nucleus.

On the day of the study, I went to the open market to buy two or three live eels. Once in the icy water, they became dormant. I made an incision around the neck, massaged the long body, and collected blood into a test tube. After the experiments, Dr. MacKay allowed me to take them home for food.

The eel's delicate meat and exquisite flavor fully justified the price tag. We often joked that God took care of poor seminarians. At that time, Ken had already quit his job, and we couldn't afford such a luxury.

He erupted into laughter. "You brought home so many eels that you stewed them, fried them, baked them... all sorts of cuisine. We also shared them with our neighbors in the dorm. After eating them nonstop for months, everyone declined to accept the freebie."

"Too bad the grant ended in three years." Our shared past brought me a grin. Then I frowned at the less pleasant thought. Our marriage hit a rough patch when I was out of work and he still had one more year to go at the seminary.

Someone knocked on my office door. Andrew, my new boss, stood outside. "Ken, I have to go. Let's talk later."

Andrew pulled out a chair to sit on and directed narrowed green eyes at me. "Ruth, I saw the manuscript you submitted two days ago for my approval. Why didn't you include me as one of the authors? Didn't I make it clear when you joined my group? Everyone in my department has to add my name if they intend to publish a paper."

I pressed my lips together. With more than a hundred scientific reports under my belt, I knew the process. To protect intellectual property, our company put strict policies and procedures in place. Each request for publication required three signatures—from the scientist's direct supervisor, the divisional vice president, and the patent attorney.

In prior groups, my managers always told me only individuals who made direct contributions should be included as coauthors. Andrew had his own rules.

Not receiving a response, my boss stood up. "If you want this paper in print, send me a revised manuscript with my name on it."

He left, and the room felt cold. I folded my arms tight across my chest.

According to the rumors Suzuki told me, Andrew was a bully and ruthless in dealing with unruly subordinates.

Should I? Or should I not?

I stood to pace around my office, the gray rubber floor softening my stomps.

What would Andrew do if I refused?

He might make my life so miserable at work that I had no choice but to quit. After being a biochemist for more than a decade, I couldn't imagine myself without a lab.

Biochemical research was an important part of me. As a hundred scenarios raced through my head, I walked out of the office toward the lab.

Suzuki and two technicians stood by the bench. Light gleamed on pipettes, test tubes, and beakers. My coworkers looked up and smiled at me. Not wanting to disturb them, I waved and trod away.

I peeked through the window in the corridor and watched the raindrops accumulating into a temporary pond. When did it start to rain?

A black bird flew by and circled back. She dipped one wing into the water, then sharply swerved up. What scared her?

Lord, is it time for me to pursue my dream?

I studied my right palm and left elbow again. If I couldn't even handle giving a speech at a university, how could I manage a new biotech company?

With my teeth boring into my bottom lip to stifle a sigh, I returned to my office and checked the clock.

Not quite eleven. Should I ask Ken to meet me at Sushi Bangkok for lunch?

After we had Jonny, we tried to have a weekly lunch date to avoid being sucked into a routine that revolved around our son. We usually met in a nearby diner on a Friday.

Today was Tuesday.

I dialed Ken's number.

Ten minutes later, we met in the crowded restaurant. The background music seemed louder than usual, but the hostess seated us in a quiet corner, the tan walls absorbing the light from a pendant fixture dangling over our table. After we placed our orders, I told Ken what'd happened. He wrapped his large hand over mine. "Tough, isn't it?"

My throat closed. "I don't know what to do."

He played with my fingers. "Remember Tony, your first boss?"

The profile of a tall, obese man with a habitual melancholy expression emerged in my mind. "Why did you bring him up?"

Yet I knew why.

Ken dipped his chin. "When you landed the entry-level position in the company, we were overjoyed. Your salary jumped three times, which allowed us to purchase our first home."

Warmth crept into my heart. "Yeah, we grew many vegetables in that small backyard."

The warmth faded away like mist dissolving in sunlight. Three months into my new job, the nightmare began when the results from my experiments didn't meet Tony's wishes.

I could almost hear his terse tone. "Your data can't be right. Do it again."

Over the next weeks, I repeated the experiments by different approaches, and the results pointed to the same conclusion. Tony's research plan had no merit. The protein we studied had nothing to do with cardiovascular disease.

Our waiter brought us two bento boxes. Ken waited for him to leave before saying, "You called me in desperation. Tony had asked you to take out the negative data and only report the ones he liked in the upcoming quarterly project review."

That phone call remained vivid. Together, we decided I should record what my boss told me. I waited until late in the afternoon to send Tony an email with a verbatim account of our conversation. The next day, not long after I settled in my chair, he walked up with a piece of paper. "You're protecting yourself too much." He threw the paper on my desk. I didn't know where my courage came from, but I stood up, stared into his blue eyes, and retorted, "What's wrong with protecting myself?"

I lapsed into silence at another distasteful memory.

Following our vile interaction, Tony stomped back to his office. He ignored me for weeks, then stopped by my cubicle one morning. "Ruth, our departmental head needs an update. You're on."

He told me the time of the meeting—only half an hour away. He'd set me up for failure.

I did a terrible job that day and cried out to God, "Lord, I need Your help. What can I do to avoid this sort of torment?"

I got an idea during my devotion. Following each study, I organized new data into slides with a written report. Thus, whenever Tony called me to the stage on a whim, I would stay prepared.

Ken patted my arm to garner my attention. "You often said if it weren't because of Tony, you wouldn't have developed the skill of assembling your results into scientific manuscripts and submitting them for publication."

"True. But I went through so much distress."

Every morning I went to work, I agonized over what new tricks Tony would use to pester me. Six months later, on the verge of a breakdown, I was ready to resign.

Like a miracle, another department contacted me for an interview. The manager, Travis, asked if I was prepared to give a talk about my current research. I flipped open my laptop and gave a brief yet comprehensive presentation. Afterward, I saw the admiration in his eyes.

My shoulders loosened up a bit. "Remember Travis? He hired me and got me out of that hostile working environment."

Ken cut his teriyaki chicken into pieces. "Indeed. Jehovah-Jireh."

"But I'm no longer an entry-level scientist. To find another suitable position in my company? Almost impossible." I savored the lightly battered crispy shrimp tempura and tamped down the urge to mention my start-up dreams. Such dreams were impractical at this juncture, and if anything, I was a practical woman. "Also, the situation isn't the same. What Tony wanted me to do was unethical. To add Andrew's name to my papers? It won't affect any patient's welfare, not even mine."

"Is it pleasing to God?"

I halted my chopsticks. "It's in a gray zone. I should add his name and resubmit my request."

Ken shook his head, the pendant light reflecting on his glasses. "If you give in now, next time he asks you to do something unacceptable, what will you do?"

I frowned. "I'll worry about it when it happens."

Chapter Fourteen

Back in Dr. Stone's office that Thursday, I showed her my right palm and left elbow.

"The cortisone shot worked. The bump went down." She examined my hand, then moved on to the other arm. "Looks like another inflamed tendon. Do you want to see the orthopedic surgeon again?"

I touched my chin. "It won't solve the problem. I need to find out the cause of the inflammation."

"Any suggestions?" Dr. Stone rocked back in her chair. "Did you start something new recently, like a vigorous exercise routine?"

Aha! I blurted out, "Must be the side effect of my medication."

"Crestor does induce muscle weakness like other statins. But tendinitis?" She scratched her forehead. "Let's try this. Stop Crestor for a few weeks and see what happens. I'll order one more blood test for you. Please schedule an appointment with the receptionist."

My heart sank. My years of training and background in the pharmaceutical industry only made the tightness in my chest more unbearable. I now faced a long period of uncertainty with numerous tests and a dire outcome.

Outside the medical building, shrubs with delicate red flowers swayed in the wind. Yet I hurried past them. With my head bent low, I plopped down on the driver's seat and prayed. "Oh, Lord, what will become of me? Does it mean I should give up the dream of setting up my biotech start-up? I can't handle so many moving pieces in my life."

The magnet near the instrument panel caught my eye with its words—*Let the wild thunder roar; together we are safe.*

Tears welled up as I smiled. *Lord, this isn't the first time I face a precarious future beyond my control.*

My cell phone rang, and as I answered, Ken's voice echoed in the car. "How is it? Are you at work?"

"I'm in the parking lot in front of Dr. Stone's building. I'm afraid a load of peril awaits me." I told him my suspicion about Crestor's side effects. "Thanks for digging out the magnet from our storage bin the other day. I'm glad I have it with me here. It reminds me of how God helped me through numerous challenges in the past. I know He is with me."

"Let the wild thunder roar. We are safe with the Lord." Ken recited in an emotional tone. "I often wonder. If God didn't intervene, we wouldn't have gotten married."

"Yeah, I told Mom the same thing." I blew him a loud kiss and started the engine. "Talk to you later. I have to get back to my office now."

"Oh, before you go, Cindy at church called me earlier today. She needs to talk to you."

I placed my purse on the passenger seat. "Cindy? Which Cindy?"

"Cindy Dong, the single mom who came to our church last month."

Yeah, a young woman with a round face and a lovely figure. Why would she want to talk to me? I hadn't had many interactions with her. "Please text me her number. I'll call her."

Cindy and I agreed to meet the next evening. Inside Starbucks, with the steamy, sweet-scented air seemingly enough to raise my cholesterol, I stole a peek at the woman. On her exposed arms, multiple faded bruises showed signs of physical abuse.

She placed a hand on the wooden table. "Mrs. Huang, thank you so much for meeting me here."

"No problem." I shifted my legs and feet, fighting the urge to bite the inside of my cheek. "Where's your little boy? Who is taking care of him for you tonight?"

She traced a finger over the table's wooden grooves. "Charlie is good friends with Benjamin, Wendy's and Frank's son. He's with them this evening."

A devoted Christian couple. They'd graduated from my seekers' class about three years ago. After they accepted Christ, they became my faithful coworkers at church.

"Wendy suggested I talk to you. She said you could help."

"What has happened?" I clutched my purse tight, my knuckles whitening in their alarmed grip. "Sorry. Please don't think I'm trying to pry. I only want to know a bit more to see if I can assist you."

Cindy's eyes glistened, so I fumbled through my purse to retrieve a packet of tissues.

"Thank you." She wiped her face. "I met my husband at a celebration party after I graduated from UC Berkeley. He's from a wealthy family, a divorcé, and older than I am. I fell for his charm, the expensive jewelry gifts he gave me, and the fancy restaurants we visited. Within three months, we were married. After our honeymoon, Seth took frequent business trips...."

She lowered her gaze. I sipped my coffee in silence, hardly tasting the pumpkin spice latte.

"Seth ran the subsidiary of his family's company in Los Angeles." She hitched a deep breath. "One day he called me from Las Vegas and told me he'd arranged for me to meet him there and asked me to bring the company's checkbook. I was eight months pregnant with Charlie."

Her voice quavered. "A woman came to our house to take me to a private jet. Someone picked me up from the airport and brought me to a club. The leader of the gang informed me Seth owed them one point two million dollars. He could leave if he paid them one million dollars."

"Over a million?" I gasped, clattering my coffee mug onto the table. "Did he get into gambling?"

She rubbed her temples. "It had been his habit for a while. Somehow, I never suspected it."

"Did he write a check?"

"He did." She flattened her wobbling lips, then puffed out a breath. "After we got home, I begged him not to gamble again. We fought, and he hit me hard. That night, I went into labor."

"Oh no." I covered my mouth and pushed aside my coffee cup. The hollowness in her eyes carved out something inside of me and I couldn't possibly swallow.

Cindy sipped her tea while I allowed her the time to calm down. "Charlie was born a little premature but healthy. Days after his birth, Seth disappeared. He didn't come home until two weeks later. We fought, and he punched me. It... became a pattern."

How horrible. A chill ran up my back.

She dabbed her damp eyes. "I placed a restraining order against him."

"Did it help? I heard it's often ignored."

"He stalked me and sent me threatening messages." She lifted her chin. "I had no choice but to leave LA."

I stroked my neck. My anxiety refused to lift as a burden for Cindy's well-being fell on me. *Lord, please give me wisdom.* "Is there anything I can do for you?"

"Seth hired an attorney and filed a lawsuit. I received a letter from the court two days ago. His goal is to lift the restraining order and also get custody of Charlie." She gaped at me. "Wendy said you know a lot of things and can help me."

Wendy overestimated my ability. Cindy needed a lawyer, not a scientist. Yet... how could I brush her aside when she needed someone to lean on? *Lord, what should I do?*

I folded my arms on the table, leaning over the wooden surface. "Cindy, are you a Christian?"

She bobbed her head. "I attended a Catholic high school but didn't understand Christianity. After I came here, I met Wendy, and she shared the gospel with me. I realized I was a gold digger. I married Seth not out of love but for money. It's a sin." Her eyes glistened once more. "I confessed all my sins. Wendy said God has forgiven me because of Jesus Christ's sacrificial death on the cross."

Praise the Lord. My shoulders relaxed, the Lord taking their burden. "I'm glad to hear that. May I pray for you?"

"Please do." She reached her hand, palm up, across the table, and I took it.

Praying in a low voice, I asked God for a resolution to Cindy's problem. After my prayer, I let go of her hand. "You need an attorney to represent you."

A crease formed between her brows. "Isn't it expensive? I don't have money."

"We have a lawyer at church. She may assist you. Also, our church has a benevolent fund for members to tide them over."

"I'm not a member yet."

I patted her arm. "I know. Still, you should apply. Maybe the deacon board will make an exception for you."

You can do more. The thought—no, the command—burst into my soul with such force that an impulse coursed through my veins. *Lord, is it from You?* "To help you get started, I can give you some money now."

I took out my checkbook and wrote five hundred dollars.

She stared at the check I placed on the table. "You hardly know me." Tears streaked her cheeks. "I don't know how to thank you. You are extremely kind, even though I can never pay you back."

"No need to thank me. Our heavenly Father has given me lots of blessings. I have no way to ever repay Him and can only pay forward." As I said those words, a scene from my past glided across my mind. Yes, I was once trapped in a desperate position, although the circumstances were different. God, via His divine way, provided me with a solution beyond my imagination.

Cindy tucked the check into her bag. "Thank you again for your help. What's the attorney's name? Can you introduce him or her to me as soon as possible?"

I jotted down Stacey Wood's name and phone number on a piece of napkin. "She is a sister in our English congregation. Call her and let her know I gave you her contact information."

After she left, I slumped back into my chair.

Lord, thank You for sending over Cindy. Thank You for reminding me of Your guidance and protection in the past.

When I organized my diaries into digital files last year, I spent hours reading my entries from a difficult period in my married life.

Closing my eyes, I pondered our dorm unit in the seminary affiliated with the Chinese University of Hong Kong.

Before the seminary admitted Ken, they only had rooms for singles. To accommodate the first married student, the school converted a storage unit and its adjacent men's restroom with its urinals and stalls into an apartment. Ken and I often joked with each other, "We never have to argue about who should go first."

Yet after I lost my job, I frowned every time I walked into the unconventional setup. Since Ken entered his third year in the Master of Divinity program, he spent most of his time in the library. I stayed home alone every day. Even with a fan, the summer warmth in that confined space became as oppressive as the gloom in my mind.

I couldn't help checking our bank account daily and muttered under my breath, "I need to find work. No way we'll ask my in-laws or my mom for money to pay our bills."

Yet how? I'd gone to so many interviews, including commission-based sales positions. I still hadn't found a job.

The survival anxiety associated with Dad's death surged up like a turbulent torrent. I was a helpless teenager back then. Now I had a doctorate.

But was there a difference?

On the table lay the most recent rejection letter. "Although we are impressed by your credentials, you are overqualified...."

Worse, whenever I considered leaving my beloved biochemistry research to do something else, anguish shot through my heart.

Didn't everyone tell me I was a gifted scientist? How could I throw away my talent?

The intense, negative feelings prompted me to complain every day. "Nobody wants me."

My husband patted my arm. "Not true. Sooner or later, you'll find a job."

"Easier said than done. When? Where?" I nearly stomped my foot, trying to rid myself of the pent-up frustration, but he shrugged and left for his studies.

Couldn't he even give me some sympathy?

With nothing to do, I strolled to the creek near our dorm and surveyed the subtropical plants. The sweet fragrance of white ginger flowers floated into my nostrils like before, but I no longer responded with a smile.

Maybe it was time for me to apply for research positions in the US. So, I broke down and sent out seven applications to different universities without Ken's knowledge. Within a few weeks, I received six offers.

On the day the value of our checking account fell below five thousand Hong Kong dollars, I sat Ken down on the sofa Mom bought for us. "I've found a job."

"Finally." He hugged me. "Is it far from home? When do you start?"

Scooting back from him, I kneaded my brows. "Very far. It's in Houston. With your permission, I plan to leave Hong Kong at the end of this month."

He blinked behind his glasses. "Houston?"

"Yes." Somehow, I kept my voice even and forced a smile. "Houston, Texas."

He pulled off his glasses and rubbed his eyes. With his hand still over them, he shook his head. "I still believe the Lord wants us to serve in Hong Kong."

I scowled. "Yeah, it sounds great. But how will we pay bills? Are you willing to quit school and return to civil engineering? If you don't, then I need to work. We have very little money left. Even for my airfare to Houston, my mom has to chip in."

Ken shifted away from me, his expression desolate. "You arranged all this without even mentioning a word to me."

I sucked in a quick breath. "I'm sorry. I didn't know whether my job search would yield anything. Plus, we've been arguing so much recently. I..."

Tongue-tied, I clenched my hands in my lap and huffed out a breath.

His face contorted. "Will you come back?"

"Of course." Without hesitation, I grasped his arm. "As soon as you graduate and start serving as an assistant pastor, I'll be back. I told my future boss I would work in her lab for only one year, and Dr. Jones has agreed."

"You have everything arranged."

His low whisper somehow hurt me. I sighed. "Don't worry. God has sovereignty over our future."

I meant it. But was it true? Or had I tried to wrest it back from Him?

As I settled into my window seat and gazed at the tarmac while the plane taxied along, one thought nagged at me—the message I'd heard the day before when I prayed about my job in Houston. "I gave biochemistry back to you after you married Ken. Will you offer it to Me again?"

That was absurd. Abraham only sacrificed Isaac once.

The silver bird took off and flew over one skyscraper after another. Soon, the islands below appeared like black dots on a blue canvas.

Moisture blurred my vision. All my buried emotions surged to the surface.

I was stepping onto an uncertain journey.

My mind turned to Mom. She not only bought the plane ticket for me but also agreed to come to Houston to help out. She was always there for me, even though she didn't agree with me and confronted me. "Have you prayed about it? You're making a mistake to leave Hong Kong by yourself."

The cabin lights dimmed.

I jammed my knees into the seat in front. *Lord, is my mom right? Will You continue to walk with me?*

Finding no easy answer, I forced myself to watch movies and drifted to sleep.

At the Houston airport, one of Ken's friends, Luna, came to take me to the residence for postdoctoral fellows. Four months later, I picked up my mother from the same airport.

Mom dropped her luggage on the bed and scowled at me. "Mimi, how could you leave your husband all alone by himself? Don't you know separation can damage a marriage?"

I ignored her question. "Didn't you say you would come to help me settle? Why didn't you come sooner?"

"I have to..." She halted when someone knocked on the door.

At ten thirty in the morning, who could be there?

I opened the door.

"Hi, Ruth." Simon, my coworker, smiled at me. "I went down to Galveston and caught a lot of fish." He raised the bag in his hand. His dark blue eyes shone. "For you. You told me you used to buy live fish from the wet market in Hong Kong."

"I..." I took the bag from him. "Thank you. Sorry, I can't invite you in. My mother has just arrived from Tokyo."

He waved at me. "Sure. No problem. See you in the lab on Monday."

A groove formed between Mom's eyebrows as I reentered the studio apartment. "Mimi, who was that?"

"A colleague." I shrugged, already hearing her response.

She crossed her arms over her chest, her eyes narrowing at me. "Why would a *male* coworker stop by on a *Saturday* morning and give you fish?"

The joy from our reunion vanished. I clenched my teeth. "Why are you interrogating me as if I've done something wrong?"

She squinted. "Have you done anything wrong?"

"Of course not." I rubbed my temples. Yet I couldn't deny Simon's interest in me flattered my ego.

Her shoulders relaxed.

"Don't you trust me?" I grasped her hand. "In our mainstream culture, many consider sex like food that we can't live without. As a Christian, I know it's a deception from the world. I understand why some men are interested in me. Without my husband by my side, they think they can..."

"I'm glad." Mom hugged me. "You're always well disciplined. I'm worried you get too confident, too cocky. The Bible is full of stories about heroes who thought they wouldn't slip. Then they fell miserably."

"Oh, Mom." I touched her shoulders, warmth sweeping over me. "Now, tell me why you didn't come earlier."

She drew me to sit on the saggy sofa. "I had a procedure done to remove stones from my gallbladder. I didn't want to come here unprepared since I don't have insurance in the US."

"Are you fully recovered?" I leaned against her bosom.

"Yes." Her tight hug jostled me. "How about you? How is your research project?"

"Going full speed." My chest swelled. I told her how I successfully purified a protein from cells and injected it into mice. "I'll have monoclonal antibodies for my studies soon."

"Your magic fingers work their wonders." She grinned, then yawned. "I'd better take a nap to adjust my jet lag."

While listening to her even breathing, I folded my arms on my knees and rested my head on them.

I didn't tell her the whole story. A week ago, Dr. Jones offered to apply for a green card, the permanent resident status, for me. She didn't want me to quit after one short year.

My heart fluttered. I wasn't sure which I felt more—excitement or unease about Ken and our future.

During our conversation, maybe sensing my hesitancy, Dr. Jones spoke in a voice gentler than usual. "You don't have to decide now, but I do need an answer in two or three months. If you still plan to leave, I'll need to put out an ad to hire your replacement."

Distinct scenarios rushed back to haunt me. I brought it before God that night. "Lord, once more, my talents as a scientist are recognized. Should I take my boss's offer?"

Will you sacrifice your Isaac to me again?

"Lord, are You telling me biochemistry has taken over Your prime position in my life? Please give me specific signs to help me make my decision."

But this time, God didn't give me any sign.

In the following weeks, my mind swung like a pendulum. One day, I would feel strong in my faith, ready to put everything aside for the Lord. The next day, I shifted to the other extreme and convinced myself my career was more important than anything else.

Trapped in a deep mire of indecision, I jotted down in my diary, "I need Your guidance. Lord, please answer me."

My letters and phone calls to Ken must have betrayed my disturbance. We argued and fought.

Mom saw through my façade. She took my arm and steered me to the sofa, then forced me to sit with her in that way only mothers can. "Mimi, what's going on? You're agitated all the time."

My breaths came in stuttered heaves as I fought to control my emotions. "Mom, I..." I bared my soul and told her everything. "I don't know what to do."

"Mimi." She pulled me into her bosom. "You can't make this decision alone. You have to tell your husband."

I heeded Mom's advice and called Ken. He remained quiet long after I finished, and I held my breath, barely enduring his silence. Then his weary baritone sounded. "Ruth, I still believe God wants us to serve in Hong Kong. I told you from the beginning. I thought you agreed."

"I..." I couldn't find my tongue. "Oh, forget it."

A phrase I read a while ago popped up. *It is easy to offer God everything when you have nothing; it is difficult to offer God anything when you own something.*

"I won't force a decision on you." Somehow, Ken's calm tone made his words harder to hear. "I'll simply love you. And I'll wait and pray."

While I continued to waver, Mom watched me struggle. By then, she knew a battle of wills waged between the Lord and me. Any word from her would aggravate the matter.

A week before I had to give a firm reply to Dr. Jones, I wrote a letter informing Ken I'd decided to stay in the US and wouldn't return to Hong Kong.

I went to the nearby mailbox, ready to drop the envelope. As I trudged forward, a potent force stopped me. I stood at the street corner and prayed. The same question flew into my head. *Will you sacrifice your Isaac to Me again?*

Tears welled up in my eyes, and goosebumps covered my arms.

I tore my letter into pieces and whispered, "Lord, yes, I will. To You, only to You."

On my way back to the apartment, I felt drowned in bittersweet feelings. Bitter because the loss of my beloved biochemistry would forever leave a vacuum in my heart. Sweet because God Himself would fill the void.

So, that must be how Abraham felt when he walked with his son to Moriah.

My memories went awry at the ring of my cell phone.

Ken's voice sounded. "Are you done with Cindy? How did it go?"

"It's complicated. I'll tell you later." I frowned, then smiled. "Through her, the Lord reminded me of our shared past. Somehow, I don't feel so worried about my cholesterol problem anymore. God will provide me with a way out."

He chuckled. "Yeah? I can't wait to hear the details."

"Sure thing." I grabbed my purse and stood. "When I plodded through the memory of those miserable days, I recalled many things but not some particulars."

"Come home and let's discuss."

Sitting in bed with Ken at night, I mentioned my conversation with Cindy brought back images of a wretched segment of our past.

"We were once in a desperate situation like her." He clasped me tight. "Although it appeared hopeless, the Lord intervened, and everything worked out well."

I nodded, warmth creeping into my heart. "I remember your application to serve at your home church ran into difficulties, but I forget the details."

A subtle agitation tightened his usually calm features. "Because my father served as the senior pastor, some congregants didn't like having his son work in the same church, while others loved it. The situation grew so bad that elders and deacons fought against one another. After many prayers, I withdrew my application."

I fiddled with a button on his pajama top. "What went through your mind when you left Hong Kong?"

"Crushing devastation. After all the trouble, the fights between us, and the instabilities, you agreed we would serve Him in Hong Kong. Then the unexpected outcome. Thankfully, God sent you to Houston ahead of me. At least I had a place to go. Still, on my flight to Houston, I felt like Abraham leaving Ur. All along, I thought God intended me to serve Him as a pastor in Hong Kong. My understanding of God's calling for me was wrong. The experience humbled me. I vowed to God that—no matter what—I'd learn to trust and obey, like Abraham."

I peered at Ken as his chest rose and fell beside me. "I'm so thankful the Lord gave me the free will to choose. Who am I in front of the Almighty God? Yet He didn't use His power to force me to surrender. He engaged in a tug-of-war game with me. God not only gave biochemistry back to me, but He also prepared a chaplain intern position for you in the Lutheran Hospital, right next to my research building."

Ken's lips eased into a smile. "I'm grateful too. That work experience enabled me to join the Christian Reformed Church in Chicago."

"Yes, God pulled us through. I'm sure He'll show His mercy to Cindy." Hearing his heart's steady thump, I sighed. "My health still concerns me. If Crestor is the culprit for my tendon problem, then I'm caught in the dilemma of choosing between two evils. The pain caused by my medication is unbearable, but the cardiovascular complications induced by high cholesterol are deadly."

"Pray. God will guide you."

Chapter Fifteen

On Saturday afternoon, I sat at the dining table in silence.

Ken tugged at my sleeve to get my attention. "What's bugging you?"

"No, nothing. I was thinking about my next appointment with Dr. Stone and what she'll suggest." I rubbed my chin. "Mrs. Yang in my seekers' class called me earlier today."

He cast me a puzzled glance. "Mrs. Yang? Mark's mother? Why did she call you?"

I moved my hand to scratch my forehead. "She has some questions and wants us to pay her a visit."

My husband kept quiet, waiting for me to continue.

I stood to pour myself a cup of water. "The first time she showed up in my seekers' class, she declared to everyone that she was an atheist. When I asked why she came to church, she frowned and muttered that her son wanted her to come."

Ken gave me an encouraging nod.

"In the beginning, she often sat with her head bent low. Was she listening or dozing off out of boredom? I couldn't tell." I crinkled up my lips. "Then I had a run-in with a visitor about Falun Gong, the popular cult in China, and Mrs. Yang surprised me by commenting that my relevant lesson helped her a lot."

"Amazing." Ken shot to his feet. "The Holy Spirit is working in her. Remember a while ago Mark Yang talked to me after our prayer meeting? He said his mom planned to visit them and begged me to pray for her salvation. He didn't wish others to know because his mom is a high-level Communist party official."

I took another gulp of water. "I sense the change in her attitude toward Christianity. Should I call her? Would tonight work for you?"

We arranged for Mom to take care of Jonny, then drove to an affluent neighborhood about fifteen minutes from us. As we stepped into the Yangs' foyer, I widened my eyes. "Wow, this place is gorgeous. How many bedrooms do you have?"

A gentle grin crooked up a corner of Mrs. Yang's mouth. "Five. In this area, this house is considered quite modest."

"Is Mark home?" Ken took off his shoes. "You must be proud of him. He's doing well in his company."

Mrs. Yang led us to the living room. "They took the children to their table tennis lesson."

We gathered around a huge, antique-looking, rosewood dining table. The hostess brought out a bowl of mixed fruit and three forks. "Mark wants me to visit them often, but I used to dread coming here."

I raised my brows.

"Although they're well off, Mark had an awful relationship with his wife and two kids." Her hand shook as she poured us tea. "Being around them brought me lots of distress."

"And then?" I accepted the cup from her and cradled the delicate china with its golden rim as tangy steam rose from it.

She leaned back in her chair. "I didn't expect to see any difference this time. Oddly enough, they've changed. They no longer quarrel and treat their two boys with respect and love."

I exchanged glances with my husband. Mark and his wife, Tina, accepted Christ as their Savior last year. The work of the Holy Spirit was astounding.

"Mark told me about Jesus. In the beginning, I was skeptical." She sipped her tea. "You probably heard about this before. In China, we're taught that religion is the people's opium. I used to believe communism would build a utopia in this world."

Used to? "How about now?"

She hesitated, turning her cup around, her frown focusing on it. "Mark said I can trust you."

We kept quiet

She put down her teacup. "I came from a poor family. I belong to the Red Five Categories. Do you know what they are?"

I shook my head.

"Poor and lower-middle peasants, laborers, revolutionary soldiers, revolutionary cadres, and revolutionary martyrs." Her shoulders hunched forward. "My father was a poor farmer. Under the rule of the Communist party, my life took a different direction for the better. In high school, I got accepted into the party and went to Peking University, the best in China. I married another high-ranking official. All I have is from the party."

She puffed out a breath. "During the Cultural Revolution, many of our friends were sent down to the remote countryside. We remained in Beijing but witnessed firsthand the persecution of Christians. I thought they deserved the punishment. After Deng Xiaoping started the reforms, we believed, this time, communism would prevail in realizing our dream of an improved world. Then the '89 Tiananmen Square Student Movement..."

Yeah, the Tiananmen Square massacre. In the previous church we served, a few in our congregation were fugitives from that horrid incident.

Not sure about how to react, I reached for my teacup.

"Sorry, I went off track." Mrs. Yang pushed the bowl toward me. "Have some fruit."

While I picked up a piece of apple, she tapped manicured nails against her cup. "Back to why I wanted to talk to you today. Mark and Tina are both communists. Communism didn't help them get along as a couple. They treated their kids as if training little soldiers. Then they became Christians and changed. I can't help asking, 'What's the force behind it?'"

I leaned forward. "Have you received your answer?"

"Thank you for your teachings at the seekers' class." She nodded to me. "They helped me develop a good idea about Christianity. Jesus didn't just pop up in history. The Old Testament prophesied His coming."

I inclined my head with approval. "I mentioned during one of the lessons that more than three hundred prophecies from the Old Testament were fulfilled in Jesus Christ."

"Indeed." She flashed a warm smile. "The book of Isaiah clearly states, 'For to us a child is born, to us a son is given, and the government will be on his shoulders. And he will be called Wonderful Counselor, Mighty God, Everlasting Father, Prince of Peace.' Isn't it amazing? The Almighty God, the Everlasting Father, would be born as a baby into the world."

While she paused, watching me with an intense gaze, I blurted out, "You memorized Isaiah chapter nine, verse six?"

"I appreciated what you said about the Dead Sea Scrolls. I did some online research myself. The book of Isaiah is one of the original seven Dead Sea Scrolls discovered in Qumran, dating from 125 BCE. It's also the largest and best-preserved of all the biblical scrolls." She reached across the table to pat my arm. "I intended to raise a question in class but felt embarrassed because the Bible teaches about creation. We were taught the evolution theory at school. Do you truly believe God created humans?"

Lord, please give me wisdom. I swallowed my mouthful of fruit before speaking. "Do you remember we discussed God's attributes in one lesson? We talked about His holiness, sovereignty, faithfulness, love, and mercy."

"Yes, I do." Mrs. Yang took a bite of a peach.

"I also emphasized some of God's attributes that are beyond our human experience and comprehension. One of them is related to time and space. While we're constrained by time, God isn't."

She stopped chewing, and her smooth forehead crinkled between her eyes.

"You're probably wondering why I brought this up." I placed my fork on the plate. "The Bible says God created the world in six days. The evolution hypothesis proposes humans and monkeys evolved from an apelike common ancestor over about six million years. If God is beyond time, then to Him there's no difference between six days and six million years. Creation and evolution both involve the element of time, but God can't be confined by time."

"Ah, I got it." Her forehead smoothed out again. "The debate between creation and evolution is unnecessary because they've both overlooked an important factor. God transcends time and space."

I nodded again. "Yes."

"One last question." She raised her index finger, maroon glinting on her nail. "Why does Genesis say that God created the world in six days?"

My eyes followed her hand, and I almost lost my focus at the sight of the magnificent chandelier above us. I lowered my gaze. "The Bible isn't a scientific textbook. Genesis uses human languages that have the constraint of time and space to convey one important fact. God created the universe. The only verse in the Bible not written in our languages is the writing on the wall in the Book of Daniel."

"I'm aware of that story. Nobody could comprehend, and Daniel translated for them." She forked up another piece of peach. "Now I also understand what you said about eternal life. You taught us last week the Bible doesn't define eternal life by time. The Gospel of John states, 'This is eternal life: that they may know you, the only true God, and Jesus Christ, whom you have sent.'"

Wow. She memorized John 17:3 too.

Ken chimed in. "Have you accepted Christ as your Savior?"

"I have." After her immediate and unequivocal reply, she frowned. "Pastor, may I ask you something? Is it okay if I don't get baptized?"

My husband sucked in a quick breath.

A satisfactory answer wasn't easy to provide. Seekers in my class told me that atheism remained at the core of communism, which clashed with Christianity. The Chinese government used tactics to punish Christians, including exile, prison sentences, and even the death penalty.

Lord, please give Ken proper words.

"I understand your concern," Ken spoke in a soothing tone. "You're worried that if you receive baptism here, you may get into serious trouble when you return to China. Am I right?"

Her chin-length hair fluttered around her cheeks as she bobbed her head.

"The baptism is a declaration that you're a member of God's family. The Bible teaches a believer shall be baptized. Yet exceptions existed even during Jesus' time. Both Nicodemus and Joseph of Arimathea were secret followers of Jesus. The Bible didn't say whether they were baptized." Ken took a sip of tea. "Do you plan to immigrate to the US in the future?"

Mrs. Yang kneaded her temple. "No. I don't speak English. In China, I get to do more activities."

Ken tapped the table with his fingers. "Please try to have fellowship with other Christians after you return to China. It's important for your faith journey. Once you find a suitable church, I think it's safer if you get baptized there."

"Really?" She slid her hand from her temple and feathered her fingers through her bangs, revealing furrows on her forehead. "How do I find a church in Beijing? Isn't it risky if others learn about my baptism?"

"We have contact with house churches in Beijing. Have you heard of them? They're also called underground churches. They meet in small groups at home and keep information private. They'll never leak the news of your baptism to outsiders. If you're interested, please let me know."

My cell phone rang. As I answered, I glimpsed the time. Almost nine.

"Mommy." Jonny's voice reached me. "When are you coming home?"

"Soon. Why don't you go to bed first? Don't wait for us."

After he hung up, I gave my husband a signal and stood up. "Mrs. Yang, I'm so glad to welcome you into God's family. Sorry, we have to leave. Let's find another time to meet again."

On our way back, I couldn't help asking Ken, "Should I talk about the cost of being a follower of Jesus in my class? Sometimes people mistake that once we become Christians, we'll enjoy trouble-free lives."

"Mrs. Yang lived through the Cultural Revolution as an eyewitness of the sufferings of Christians. She has a bona fide concern. You and I have never gone through that sort of horror." His lips set as the car glided to a halt before a stop sign. "Let's continue to pray for her. With the guidance from the Holy Spirit, she will make the right decision."

Ken had a valid point. *Lord, I'm not qualified to tell her about the cross we have to carry as believers.*

***

Eight days later, on Sunday afternoon, I opened the French door to step into our yard. The late summer breeze must have shifted, sweeping a pleasant scent from our neighbor's shrubs into my nostrils. Was that a seven-son flower?

As I brushed away loose strands of hair and tucked them behind my ears, Mom's voice sounded behind me. "Mimi, did you get this at church today?" Coming up beside me, she waved a piece of paper.

I cringed, my shoulders tightening up. "I did."

"Have you read it?" She pulled over a lawn chair to sit down.

I took a seat beside her. "I threw it away."

Her eyebrows spiked. "Do you know its content?"

"Ken and I have received similar letters before." Moisture clouded my vision. Why did it still hurt? We'd decided not to let anonymous attacks bother us. "Someone must be unhappy about how we do certain things at church and trying to warn others about our transgressions."

"You ought to read it."

"I can guess what's in it. Number one—the pastor and his wife love money. They only visit wealthy members and ignore the poor. Number two—the pastor's wife chooses a secular job over a Christian service. She's more concerned about her worldly accomplishments than people's souls. Number three—the pastor doesn't have leadership skills, his sermons are terrible, and he doesn't spend enough time in preparation. Number four—the pastor's family often takes luxurious cruise vacations, and the pastor doesn't respond to emails when he travels." I blinked. Still, tears wet my cheeks. "Do I need to continue?"

"Not in that order. Quite close, though." The breath she blew out ruffled her smoothed-back hair. "Do the accusations have any merits?"

I hitched a breath. "There's some truth in it. My personality *is* flawed. I can't control my tongue and like to speak my mind. I may have offended many people unintentionally."

"You've never mentioned your run-ins with church members." She frowned.

The sun warming me, I tilted my face toward the sky dotted with cotton-like white clouds. "At the first church we served, we had lunch together every Sunday following worship. A middle-aged accountant often brought five Tupperware containers to pack food for her workdays. One day, I told her to wait until everyone had eaten, then she could pack as much as she wished. She grew angry and screamed at me with a group of congregants surrounding us."

Mom touched my hand. "How did you respond?"

I fixed my gaze on a puppy-shaped cloud, detecting a pang of sorrow in its big eyes. "I didn't know what to do. Walking away would enrage her more, so I listened to her rants about my lack of love and concern for others. After about ten minutes, I asked, 'Are you done? May I leave now?'"

"Oh, Mimi." Mom patted my arm, her eyes moistening. "But I understand she felt insulted when you told her in front of a group of people that she had to wait."

"I learned my lesson." I stretched out my legs. "Nowadays, I keep my mouth shut and wait for the right opportunity to share my thoughts."

She dipped her chin. "How about Ken? He's gentle and caring, less intense than you, and isn't judgmental like you."

"In many ways, Ken has a higher EQ than me." I nodded. "Still, some congregants think he's too laid-back and lacks charisma."

"It's impossible to please everyone." She waved, batting the comment away. "My pastor in Tokyo has also received unsigned letters, although they were sent only to him, not to everybody. He called them 'suggestion letters.' He even told us a joke about one such incident. Someone sent him a note with only one word: Fool. He quipped, 'How interesting. This person signed his name and forgot to write the message.'"

Her words comforted my heart and soothed my turmoil. "I remember him. Pastor Cheng, right? I met him when I visited you. He has such a great sense of humor."

"Yeah. He's a wonderful pastor but can't be immune to anonymous complaints." She raked through her hair. "What will you and Ken do about it?"

"I need to discuss it with him." I gripped the armrest. "Most likely, he'll ask me to pray with him and wait for our deacon board to investigate."

"Okay. I'll also pray for you." She pushed to her feet and strolled back to the house.

I lifted a silent prayer. *Lord, is it wrong for me to pursue my biochemistry career?*

If I set up my biotech start-up, would it lead to more criticism from church members? What about those days when I engaged in a tug-of-war game with God over my love of biochemistry? Hadn't I learned my lesson?

A hand fell on my shoulder. I raised my head, and Ken stood in front of me. "Ruth, I'm sorry the letter also targets you."

"We're in the same boat. There's no escape." I gestured for him to sit. "I'm a coward. I didn't read it."

"Tossing it away and ignoring its contents isn't an option for me." He took the empty lawn chair. "Accusations have been made. You and I know most of them are groundless, but they're dangerous because they arouse doubts in others."

I stole a peek at his somber expression, his eyes sad behind his thick glasses. "What's your plan? Will you say something about it to the congregation next Sunday?"

"I'll have to. All the people who have received it will expect a response from me." He rubbed his neck. "The person did raise some excellent points. I haven't provided a clear outreach focus for our church. I can see why he or she is concerned. If we don't take the gospel to those outside us, our church will dwindle and fade away. Another accusation is also right on. Our discipleship programs aren't effective. We need to establish a culture to help newcomers and regulars deepen their level of maturity."

He sounded so calm. I puffed out a breath—and the question. "Don't you feel angry?"

"When I first read it, I got indignant. I wanted to retaliate." He straightened his spine and steepled his fingers before him, tapping them together in his contemplative pose. "After I kneeled in my office and prayed, the Lord opened my eyes. I recalled a lesson I learned from counseling courses at Trinity. Conflicts with others, if not dealt with properly, can hurt everyone involved. But if we handle conflicts with mercy, love, and grace from the Lord, they can become opportunities for building up one another. Satan is using one of us to attack God's church. If I fight back, I'll fall into the enemy's trap. The only way to handle this is to pray and wait on the Lord."

Heat rose to my throat. I swallowed hard. "You sounded like preaching a sermon. That won't be sufficient. You'll need to take some specific steps. Praying and waiting on the Lord won't solve the problem unless God does a miracle to make the anonymous writer step forward and apologize."

"Such a miracle rarely happens." He crooked up his mouth into a tentative smile. "You're right, though. I've already talked to a few deacons from the Chinese congregation, and the deacon board will meet tomorrow evening. With their permission, during next Sunday's sermon, I'll thank the author for the constructive criticism. The deacon board will also outline a plan to address the outreach and discipleship-training issues."

I touched my forehead. "What if the letter is from one of our key leaders?"

He lapsed into silence, then shook his head. "I don't think so. Even if it's from one of the leaders, the approach should still work."

"How will you deal with the personal attacks like my ambition and your bad sermons?"

"Let's consider those as a reminder from the Lord that we're far from perfect. We rely on His mercy to serve Him."

Another breeze swept past, and a whiff of a different scent surprised me. What was it? Didn't smell like the seven-son flower anymore. I massaged my temples. "Do you think Jonny may be impacted? Will some kids at church mock him?"

"He seemed fine when I saw him a while ago." Ken drew his brows tight. "I'll talk to him."

The mention of Jonny led me to another concern. "Mom told me we overload Jonny with extracurricular activities. Do you think so?"

Ken scrunched his nose, then pushed his glasses back up. "Mom has got a good point. Maybe we should drop one of his after-school programs? How about the one with a focus on math? Jonny's math is already very good."

Math? Math was his best subject. He had such potential if he chose to pursue it.

"No, not math!" I curled my hands into fists. "Maybe art. He isn't interested in art, anyway."

Chapter Sixteen

The next Saturday, I sat at my desk in my home office, my computer screen blurring as I lost focus. The dread inside of me—the fear I'd been holding in since Dr. Stone told me the news—broke free.

What would happen to me?

Three days ago, Dr. Stone had looked calm as she laced her fingers in her lap and delivered her news. "All your cholesterol indexes are again way out of the normal range. I'm afraid you have no choice but to go back to Crestor."

My throat had closed, and my voice cracked. "How about my tendon problem? Can I try another statin?"

My doctor shook her head, the obvious sympathy in her eyes nearly undoing me. "You did worse with the other medications I gave you. Although tendinitis is painful, at least it won't kill you."

A buzz pulled my attention back to the present. A fly zipped past me.

When did it get in?

I waited for it to land on my leg and slammed my palm down on its body.

Eww! I should have smashed it with something else.

I removed the dead bug with sanitary wet wipes, yet couldn't mop away the feeling of helplessness.

Was every one of us, like this fly, an accidental existence in an accidental world? If my cholesterol level remained high, would a heart attack kill me soon? Then what would happen to my mother, husband, and son?

Should I accept the excruciating pain brought on by Crestor or prepare to die of cardiovascular complications?

Perhaps Dr. Stone didn't err. I had no choice.

A soft voice emerged within me. *Pray. You can always pray.*

I rubbed my temples. *Oh, Lord, I've been praying about it since my doctor's visit. I still don't know what to do.*

A hymn—"I Know Who Holds Tomorrow"—sang into my thoughts. Okay, one last attempt.

In the Google search box, I typed in, "Mayo Clinic, statin side effects." A page came up with the title "Statin side effects: Weigh the benefits and risks."

Same old, same old.

I threw up my hands.

Muscle pain, liver damage... but nothing about tendon problems.

I scowled at the screen, and a sentence caught my eye. "Change your dose..."

"Mimi, where are you?" Mom called from the hallway. "In your office?"

She leaned against the doorpost, a blue dress draping around her plump frame. "What're you doing?"

"Searching for information to learn more about my rare condition caused by statins." I closed the laptop lid.

She came forward and grasped my arm. Her gaze fell on the visible bump on my left elbow. "You went back on Crestor for less than a week, and your tendon swelling seems worse."

I offered a curt smile. "Before you walked in, I'd just seen something that may help me." I told her about a possible adjustment to the drug's dosage. "I can't do it blindly, though. I need an evidence-based approach."

"How?" Deep furrows lined her forehead.

"I don't know yet. Has Ken left with Jonny for the piano lesson?" I stood and peered at the door. "Didn't you say you want to have a dim sum in Chinatown? Let's go."

***

Patrons packed the restaurant. Yeah, Saturday.

Luckily, we got seated right away.

I placed the menu before Mom and ignored the noise from diners at the next table. "Do you want the usual?"

We always had BBQ pork bun, shrimp dumplings, steamed ribs, beef meatballs, and stuffed eggplant.

She pointed at the picture of coconut pudding. "How about this?"

"It's not good for you." I pinched my brows tight.

She moved down to another photo. "This looks delicious."

"Egg tarts? Also packed with sugar." I narrowed my eyes to suppress my bubbling annoyance. "I'll order stir-fried snow pea shoots with garlic instead."

She pressed her lips until they whitened.

I gave the waitress my slip with the ticked boxes. "Mom...?"

Taking no notice of me, she directed her gaze toward the wall-mounted TV.

I breathed in the pleasant aroma swirling around the room and leaned back against my seat. Still not hearing any response from her, I took out my cell phone to search for at-home cholesterol test kits.

Bingo.

A page from Amazon.com popped up. "Analyzer Starter Cholesterol Kit with Three Cholesterol Test Strips."

"Exactly what I need." My voice cracked with excitement as I thrust the phone to Mom.

She hesitated, then took it from me. "What is it?" Icicles fringed her tone.

"I have to monitor my cholesterol at home if I want to adjust my medication dosage." I tapped the table with my fingers. "This ought to do it. I just need to confirm the test's accuracy."

"Amazing." She gave the phone back to me. "You can find the needed information in a few clicks."

"Yeah, smartphones are powerful." I flashed her a grin. "Why don't you get—"

The waiter placed our orders before us.

Mom snatched up a BBQ pork bun with her chopsticks. "It's too complicated for me. I have a phobia of technology."

"The phone will enrich your life. You can watch TV, podcasts, and do many other activities." I chewed on a piece of rib. The tender meat melted in my mouth.

Nice to enjoy dim sum. Too bad we lived fifty miles north of Chinatown.

She didn't respond but attacked each dish with the zest of a generous appetite, as if she'd just come from a famine.

"Seriously, you ought to get a cell phone." I sampled the green leaves. Wow, nice. Garlic added a punch to the mild snow pea shoot flavor. "How about the answering machine I gave you? Have you set it up?"

She brought a hand to her mouth and yawned.

Okay, she was still angry with me. I'd better keep quiet.

I signed into my Amazon account and ordered the test kit, together with a pill slicer. To save money, I opted for free delivery.

"Done."

I glanced up. All plates were empty except my half-eaten meatball.

Mom sauntered to the restroom. I paid and trod outside to wait. After she came out, she walked past me.

"Where are you going?" I followed her into the Asian market next door.

She grabbed a shopping cart and walked down the aisle. I picked up three boxes of tofu.

As I put the items into her cart, I noticed something unusual. "What's that?"

"Golden dragon fruits."

I checked the price tag. "Whoa, ten ninety-nine a pound? More expensive than filet mignon?"

"So what? I'll pay." She pushed the cart away from me.

I trekked behind her. "What does it taste like? I bet it's sweet and bad for you."

She glared at me. "Are you concerned about me or money?"

"Both." Oops. I cringed.

"Stop being a helpless orphan." Mom spoke with clenched teeth, fire flashing in her gaze. "You live your life as if you were still a tutor in college. You won't buy any luxurious things unless they're on sale or you have coupons for them. You buy clothes from Goodwill for Jonny and yourself. When Ken purchases new shirts, you give him a hard time."

I blew out a hasty breath. "You're exaggerating. Didn't I take you on a cruise?"

She pointed a finger at me. "You booked the cheapest cabin. Without the long dress I gave you, you would have worn the same ugly gray outfit that you found from the Salvation Army a few years ago."

People nearby directed their gazes at us to watch the commotion.

I scratched my chin and lowered my voice. "Mom, I view everything, including my life, as being entrusted to me temporarily. I try to be a good steward for the Lord."

"Sounds spiritual, doesn't it?" A wry smile bunched up her cheeks and crinkled up her eyes. "God adorns the lilies of the field, which are here today and gone tomorrow. But your behavior shows me you're a chronic worrier. Your mindset is stuck in those years when we struggled for survival."

She seized the fruit from the cart and went to the cashier.

Breathe. Calm down. I hunched my shoulders. *Oh, Lord, is my mom right?*

I trudged outside and squinted into the clear blue sky. The earlier clouds had moved out. From the corner of my eyes, I sighted a chubby figure bending over a grove of hydrangeas. "Mom, I'm sorry."

She straightened up. "What took you so long? Let's go home."

***

In the morning I received the package from Amazon, I called Dr. Stone's office to ask for more blood work. Within a few days, I had two cholesterol results. The one from the lab showed 176, and the other from my analyzer was 182.

Not bad.

Mom sank into the chair beside me, her head cocked toward the results. "Looks like you're conducting a study on yourself. What's your plan?"

"I need to slice the five-milligram tablet into two and try it for four or five days. If my cholesterol is still under two hundred, I'll further reduce it to one-quarter." I placed one pill into the slicer, then slammed the lid down.

Two weeks later, early in October, I sat by the dining table with Mom and pricked my finger with a disposable lancet. Shortly after I inserted the strip into the analyzer, a number appeared: 174.

I leaped to my feet. "It worked. My cholesterol is below two hundred. I only have to take one milligram of Crestor."

Mom grasped my arm to examine the bump on my elbow. "It seems smaller."

I chuckled. "Yeah. Praise the Lord. I'm no longer caught between two evils."

She touched my shoulder, her lips spreading up with her enormous grin. "Mimi, you're so smart. I wonder how many people with your condition could have done what you did."

"Hey, my training isn't in vain." I danced a few steps away from her. "I'm free. Now I can travel without worrying about tendinitis. I'll call Dr. Nelson next Monday and let him know I'm available to give a seminar for his department. It won't be this fall, but I'm sure he can schedule me for next spring."

"Talking about travel, I'll leave for Tokyo at the end of this month." Mom drew me to sit back down. "Will you accompany me to Taiwan next March?"

"What for? Aren't you coming at the end of April like always?" I scratched my cheek, a tightness pinching my chest.

"I used to participate in the grave-sweeping festival on the Remembrance of Ancestors Day every year. Somehow, I missed it this year." She wiped her face with the back of her hand. "When did you last visit your father's grave site? It'll be nice if you can come with me next year."

My smile vanished as I thought about all the arrangements to take an overseas trip. "But—"

"Don't you have a lot of vacation days?" She waved at me. "If you're worried about the airfare, I'll pay for you."

I almost rolled my eyes. Seriously, she was pushing the money issue again? "It's not about money. I do have vacation days. Even so, I need to ask my boss and plan in advance."

"Well, it's only October. You have months to prepare." She gave my arm a playful pinch. "Join me in Tokyo first. We can fly to Taiwan together."

While I kept silent, she spoke again. "Are Ken's parents coming to visit you later this year? Don't they come every year like me?"

"No." I brushed aside a stray wisp of hair. "My sister-in-law is taking them to Europe. They won't come this year."

"Ha, Europe. Remember our trip together to London before you had Jonny? So enjoyable. I hope next year we'll have another wonderful trip together to Taiwan."

I waved a hand. "We went beyond London and traveled to Amsterdam, Brussels, Heidelberg, and many other cities in Western Europe."

She flashed a timid grin. "I still remember the vast sunflower patch in Southern Italy. Such an amazing sight to behold. And you picked a Taiwanese-speaking tour group for us. I understood everything the guide told us."

"Yeah. You became good friends with some people on our tour." My mouth curved up at the fond memories.

"Mimi, I've never asked you this before. How's your relationship with your in-laws? Originally, they also objected to Ken's courtship with you."

Why did she bring *that* up?

I patted her arm. "Don't worry. They treat me well. In the beginning, my Cantonese was limited, and we had difficulties in our communication. Nowadays, we can share our ideas. They're both matured Christians and have taught me a lot about our shared faith."

"I'm glad." As if thinking of something urgent, she left the kitchen and hurried into her room. She returned with a cloth bag, pulled out a scarf, and laid a few items on it. "This is a picture of my mother, the only one left. Your aunt trashed all the others." She pointed at a small picture. "I asked a shop to make an enlarged duplicate of it. It now hangs in my apartment."

At the mention of that long-ago incident, pain zipped through my heart. So many years ago. Why did it still hurt?

Pushing aside my emotions, I studied the black-and-white photo of a beautiful woman adorned with jewelry. "Wow, look at the jade bracelets on her wrists. I didn't know your mother came from a wealthy family."

"Yes, very rich. Although her parents didn't want her to marry my father, she insisted." Her eyes glistened. "Too bad she died young. I often wonder how my life would have been if she'd lived."

"Oh, Mom." I gave her shoulder a gentle squeeze.

"I'm okay. Thank you." She dabbed her cheek with a Kleenex, then showed me a necklace with a cross pendant. "A gift from your dad after I gave birth to you. I used to own lots of jewelry. After your dad passed away, I pawned them away one by one, except for this one. I want to save it for you, as a remembrance of your dad."

She hung the necklace around my neck, and I touched the cross engraved with flowers. "It's heavy."

"Made of platinum." One corner of her mouth tugged up. "Your dad wasn't a Christian when he gave me this. I got upset because I wanted a Buddha. Our folk religion governed my behavior back then. Now I think about it. The Lord called us before we sought Him. I'm glad your dad gave me the cross."

The metal cross warmed beneath my fingertips. Parts of me warmed as well, even as others chilled with a tinge of fear. "Are you giving it to me now? Why?"

She gripped my chin, tipping my face up to hers as she stood over me, then bent in and kissed my forehead. "Since I live in a retirement home, the manager and some workers have access to my room. When I travel, I take valuables with me just in case. This time, I decide to leave all my treasures here with you."

She directed my attention toward the other items. "You already know about the ring and the brooch." She picked up a pair of huge, old scissors to inspect it. "Because my stepmother gave birth to four children, my father shouldered a hefty burden to keep the family fed. When I married your dad, the only dowries were a quilt and a pair of scissors. The quilt got damaged, but this is still in good condition."

A piece of junk. I bristled. "You lug the scissors back and forth between Tokyo and Chicago every year?"

"Yes." She ran a finger along the scissors handle. "Now, before I leave Chicago, can you take me to Costco? I'll need to buy some vitamins as gifts for my church friends."

Chapter Seventeen

Familiar footsteps echoed in the hallway. Andrew halted outside my door. "Great. You're in your office." He entered and pulled out a chair to sit. "I stopped by earlier and didn't see you."

I rocked back in my chair. "I was in the lab."

He broke eye contact. "You've been with the company long enough. You should know well about the process of our annual performance review."

What? Was he serious? Didn't we conduct our performance review in March? It was only October.

While I kept quiet, he coughed and laced his hands together in his lap. "I know it's still early. But the guideline is that you can't wait till the last minute to tell your subordinate he doesn't perform. Every department must identify poor performers each year. I took a look recently. Suzuki is my first pick. Starting today, you need to talk to him about his poor performance."

Heat crept into my chest. I knew the process well. If an employee received a lousy performance rating for two consecutive years, he would be fired. But Suzuki? One of the best researchers I'd ever encountered. His data were always accurate.

I straightened my back and swallowed hard. "Suzuki's performance has been excellent. Before we joined your department, he received the highest rating continually. He hasn't lapsed. Everyone appreciates his work ethic and his outstanding data."

Andrew inclined his head, then wagged a finger at me. "I don't care what he used to have. In my department, having good data isn't enough. Suzuki lacks communication skills. He can't give a proper update about his results. Think about it and let me know your decision."

The ice in his voice skittered down my spine. Yet I understood his point. Suzuki spoke English laced with a heavy Japanese accent.

After Andrew left, I paced around my office, then dialed Ken's number and told him what'd happened. "We all know Andrew is a bully. To be honest, I fear for Suzuki and myself."

Ken's audible sigh reached my ears. "I probably shouldn't say this. Since you gave in to his unreasonable request and added his name to your papers, I suspect he'll demand you do something unacceptable again."

I couldn't find my tongue and twirled my hair around my finger instead.

Ken spoke in my silence. "We try to honor God in whatever we do. It isn't easy. But you shouldn't give in because you're afraid. I will pray for you and ask the Lord to give you courage and wisdom." He paused. "By the way, did you tell your boss you need to take a few hours off? Mom's flight is at three. We need to take her to the airport before one o'clock."

Oops. I forgot to tell Andrew. "No worries. I'll send him an email."

Andrew's email pinged mine with an immediate response. "Sure. Just make sure your work is done and you have enough vacation time to cover your absence."

***

As I entered the house, Mom scurried to the dining room with a plate of pork chops.

"No wonder it smells so good." I sucked in the mouthwatering aroma. "You shouldn't cook today. You're leaving this afternoon."

Her lips curved up into an enormous smile. "Not only have I cooked, but I've also prepared frozen food for you."

She opened the freezer door, and I gawked at the trays of grilled chicken and baked fish stacked on top of one another.

Ken walked in. "We don't have to cook for the entire month."

"Okay, time for lunch." Mom took her seat. "Let me say grace today."

Wow. She had never wanted to pray aloud. Why had she changed?

She bowed her head and spoke in Taiwanese. "Lord, thank You for Your blessings. Please give us Your mercy and protection. I particularly want to pray about tomorrow's congregational meeting at church. Please give the deacon board wisdom to resolve the issue in a way that will honor You. Please give Ken and Mimi the humility to accept criticism...."

Moisture gathered behind my eyelids. A thousand images of Mom flashed across my mind—her touch, her embrace, her love, and her unique ways of expressing care toward me. As tender moments from long ago flooded me, I blinked away my tears and smiled.

Her loud amen snapped me back to the present. She wagged a finger at me. "Why do you sport such a silly grin?"

"I'm a bit surprised." I raised my chopsticks to hide my emotions. "You pray very well, though."

I translated for Ken, and he clamped a hand on her shoulder, jostling her. "Yeah, Mom. Next year when you come, you ought to say grace more often."

After lunch, Mom patted the corners of her lips with a napkin, then rose and strolled to her room.

I trailed her. Eying her neatly packed bags, I picked up the largest one. "Wow, it's heavy."

Ken took it from me. "Almost twelve twenty. Let's go."

After we dropped off Mom's luggage at the airport, I grasped her hand. "Let's call each other at least once a week. I'll call you on Fridays at six, which is around eight on Saturdays in Tokyo."

"Don't forget to make arrangements so we can go to Taiwan together next March." Her cheerful red dress matched the lilt in her voice. Her tone sounded happy, but the shadow in her eyes said otherwise.

My chin dropped to my chest. Hadn't we gone through this before? Why did sadness flood me every time she left me?

Tears burning the backs of my eyes, I kneaded my brows to prevent them from falling. "Try to take a walk every day. Don't eat—"

An announcement echoed throughout the departure area.

Was there a gracious way to say goodbye to the love of your life? I swallowed my unsaid words about sweets and flung my arms around her neck. "Please take good care of yourself."

She patted my back. "There's a time for everything. Isn't that what the Bible teaches?"

A second call for the same passenger resonated around us.

Ken's subdued voice reached my ears. "Mom needs to get going lest she be late."

I translated for her, and she pulled away from me.

Goodbye. I love you. The words stayed in my brain.

She walked toward the security checkpoint and waved. Years of memories drowned me until I couldn't see anything around me.

Ken tapped my shoulder. "We'd better go. Jonny will be home soon."

"See you next March," I muttered under my breath.

***

The next morning, I entered the sanctuary and took a seat in the last pew to scrutinize the assembly. Ken sat with Pastor Terri and Pastor Rich up in the front. As usual, Frank and Wendy occupied the second pew to the left while Mark and his wife, Tina, were right behind them.

I searched for the one who might have written the anonymous note, yet knew my attempt was in vain. Maybe from a nonmember? Then he or she wouldn't be here.

Scott Warren and Joe Chen walked toward the lectern.

Scott spoke in English. "On behalf of the deacon board, I would like to thank each of our members who made the effort to participate in today's meeting."

He signaled for Joe to translate for him. They reviewed the church's bylaws, and Scott said, "The deacon board has examined each of the accusations in the letter with great care. We concluded a majority of them were groundless. However, since every one of you has received the letter, we want to allow you an opportunity to voice your thoughts. Now the platform is open to all of you. Please raise your hand, and someone will pass you the microphone. Joe will translate for you."

Wendy stood up. "The letter said the pastor and his wife love money. It's nonsense...." She pressed a palm to her chest as she choked with emotions.

Frank took the microphone from her. "My wife gets emotional easily." He talked in a calm, even voice. "I'll finish for her. Mrs. Huang is thrifty and never wastes money. She isn't shy in telling others she gets all her clothing from Goodwill and the Salvation Army. Wendy has gone with her sometimes. The practice has saved me a bundle. Instead of buying a jacket for two hundred dollars, Wendy paid ten dollars for a brand-new coat at Goodwill last winter." He paused at the giggle of several women. Then he lifted his chin. "But Mrs. Huang is generous toward others. Each year, many of us receive free cucumbers, chives, zucchinis, and other fresh produce from her garden. A few weeks ago, Wendy introduced a newcomer to Ruth. Even though she barely knew the person, upon learning of her difficulties, Ruth gave her a check of five hundred dollars—on the spot."

I blinked and soaked up his words. *Lord, I hadn't expected Cindy to share my insignificant act with them.*

After Frank sat, Steve, one of the deacons, shot to his feet. "Many of you know my wife had meningitis two years ago and almost died. But do you know I called Pastor Ken at one o'clock in the morning when our local hospital decided to transfer her to Rush's neurology center? I grew so desperate and needed someone by my side. Pastor Ken came right away. He stayed with me all night, praying with me and comforting me. Afterward, when I tried to give him a gift card, he declined and said, 'Every pastor in my position would have done the same for you.'"

Moisture clouded my eyes, but I held back my tears. That incident remained vivid in my mind. I worried about them so much that I prayed all night.

Alice, an accountant and the church's treasurer, asked for the microphone. "I'm a straight shooter like Mrs. Huang. Both of us are outspoken and opinionated. We have run-ins from time to time."

My heart sank. Distinct thoughts came in and out of focus, along with our last conflict over a bounced check.

She faced my direction. "Today, I want to speak in her defense. I'm also a career woman, a mom, and a wife. Trying to balance my many roles is like juggling fire sticks daily. Besides, Ruth has the role of being a pastor's wife. In my opinion, she's doing a wonderful job as a successful scientist at work, a doting mother at home, and a strong partner for Pastor Ken. She also teaches Sunday school, sings in the choir, and leads small groups. Of course, she's far from perfect. She can be judgmental and sometimes utters harsh words. But who of us is perfect?"

I hugged my arms across my chest at the potent urge to rush over and hug her. Yet knowing impulsivity didn't help, I remained quiet in my seat and listened.

Alice continued. "Talking about luxurious trips, don't we all take cruise vacations? Why is it a problem? Whoever wrote the letter held a double standard. And about the matter of drinking beer during a wedding rehearsal last year? Don't we all drink occasionally? Didn't Jesus turn water into wine at a wedding? The Bible teaches us we shouldn't get drunk. Some Christians give it a legalistic distortion and develop a holier-than-thou spiritual superiority. In my opinion, self-righteousness is a sin. The Pharisees at Jesus' time were full of it, and the Lord was critical of them. If the Lord comes back today, I bet He'd have issues with the legalists just like before."

Alice sat and rose again. "I forgot to mention something. Because Ruth's company covers a large portion of her family's health insurance—almost ten thousand dollars annually, the church pays less than three thousand for Pastor Ken, which is significantly less than the twelve thousand we have to pay otherwise."

The room lapsed into silence until Mark approached the lectern. "In my company, I'm responsible for setting up strategies. The process requires us to think about the entire business and its direction. Since I got baptized a year ago, I occasionally apply my training to analyze our church's situation. If you would allow me to provide some of my observations, I'd like to say that, as an organization, we have a well-defined vision that guides our strategies. The three pastors and our deacons, our leadership team, maximize their particular leadership skill sets and function effectively together. They also work hard to train new leaders. I'm glad I belong to a healthy church."

Once Mark sat, Scott faced the congregation. "During the past two weeks, the deacon board has investigated the two important points in the letter with great effort. The author pointed out correctly that our church hasn't done enough about outreach and discipleship training. However, these are not Pastor Ken's problems alone. The leadership team as a whole has to own them."

He coughed and sipped from his water bottle. "After many discussions, we've made a tentative plan. We'll expand our Sunday school classes and structure them like college courses such as 101, 201, and so on. This new system will start in the next quarter. In addition, we've formed an outreach committee. The first step is to contact the numerous seminary students who used to attend our church when they studied at Trinity and who now serve as missionaries. We'll set up a mission fund to support them financially. Furthermore, we'll evaluate their needs for short-term mission teams and send brothers and sisters to help them per their requests."

The meeting was adjourned right before noon. Walking out of the sanctuary, I grasped Wendy's hand. "I didn't know Cindy told you about our meeting and the check. How is she doing? I haven't had a chance to talk to her recently."

Wendy pulled me to a corner. "She's doing well. The deacon board approved her application for our benevolent fund, even though she isn't a member yet. Our small group also pitched in and raised money for her. Stacey Wood did a good job of representing her. I believe she'll win the custody battle."

"That's great news." I grinned, a wave of energy surging through me. "I'm thankful it turned out well for her."

Steps away from us, Frank waved at his wife. Wendy let go of my hand. "I'd better go now. We need to pick up Benjamin from his tennis lesson."

Before I had a chance to move, Mark came over and gave me a gift bag. "Mrs. Huang, my mother is going back to Beijing this afternoon. She wants me to thank you and Pastor Ken for your help. Here is a little something from her."

Don't accept gifts from congregants. My immediate concern prompted me to hand the item back to him. "Mark, please thank your mom for me, but I can't accept it."

"I understand." He pushed the bag toward me again. "My mom will be disappointed if I bring this back to her." He opened it to reveal a scarf. "I'm sure it won't cause any trouble for you. You've helped my mom so much. She's getting baptized once she returns to Beijing. This is a small token to show her appreciation."

Women nearby directed their gazes toward us. Heat crept up to my cheeks. The back and forth of the gift bag was attracting people's attention. I tucked it into my purse. "Okay, please send her my regards. We'll continue to pray for her."

On our way to pick up Jonny from Auntie's house, I closed my eyes and leaned my head against the headrest. "Looks like a rather satisfactory resolution."

"It's not resolved yet." Ken's tight tone drew my focus. "Having ideas is one thing. Execution is a different matter. If we can't carry out our plan, I expect to receive another anonymous letter next year."

"After today's meeting, I feel humbled and also encouraged." I fingered Mrs. Yang's scarf, now in my lap, the delicate red silk slipping between my hands. "You're right—we have to honor God in whatever we do. I need to think about how to deal with my boss regarding Suzuki."

A chill ran down my spine. *Lord, if I must give up my beloved biochemistry, so be it.*

Who said it was easy to follow Christ?

Chapter Eighteen

Early December 2010

Ten fifty. I twisted the landline cord between my fingers. Why didn't Mom answer her phone?

Ken's voice arose from the kitchen. "Ruth, aren't you ready for bed? You're usually asleep before ten thirty."

"I don't know what's going on. I've been calling Mom since we finished dinner." I walked to him.

He grasped my hand. "Maybe she went out with friends and forgot you call on Fridays."

"So unlike her." I chewed my lip and dialed again.

The phone rang for a long minute. No one picked up. As I replaced the receiver, an eerie hush stretched across the space in the living room.

My husband broke the silence. "Nothing you can do. Go to sleep and try to reach her tomorrow morning."

"How about you?"

He gave my arm a gentle squeeze. "Not yet. I haven't finished my sermon."

I lay flat under the bedsheet and gazed at the ceiling. A headache developed, thumping against my temples. I whispered a prayer in darkness, "Lord, please protect my mom."

The clock struck twelve. Then the phone rang. I jumped up from bed and groped for the light switch. My steps faltered. I gave up and rushed into the living room. Ken was talking on the receiver.

"Is it from Mom?" I hurried to his side.

He waved at me. "I understand. I'll talk to Ruth. We'll tell you once we finalize our plan."

"Who called? What plan?" I spoke in such a loud voice that my heart skittered.

He guided me to the sofa and gestured for me to sit. "Heidi called from Tokyo. Mom is in the hospital."

My legs quivered, and I slumped onto the sofa, bracing myself for his next sentence.

Ken crossed to my side, his shadow falling over me. "This won't be easy to hear. Mom had a stroke in her sleep. In the morning, her retirement home didn't detect any motion from their monitor system. So, they broke into her unit and found her unconscious."

Tears welled up, and I covered my face with both hands.

His warm palm rested on my shoulder. "Heidi gave me the hospital's phone number. We can contact them, but will need a translator. Do you think Suzuki in your lab can help?"

I raised my head toward the clock. Not even one thirty. "In the middle of the night?" I muttered, my voice barely audible.

Ken tugged me into his arms. "I told Heidi at least one of us will go to Tokyo as soon as possible. Do you want to call United Airlines? You always make our travel arrangements."

My feet blurred in my vision, my throat closed, and I couldn't even shake my head.

He loosened his hold on me and trod away. When he returned, he hugged me again. "I won't let you go alone. I've booked two tickets for us. We'll leave this Sunday afternoon. Jonny can stay with my aunt's family. With such short notice, it's impossible to find another pastor to preach next Sunday. We'll need to be back on Saturday."

I couldn't stop crying and pulled my legs tight against my chest. Time seemed to stretch on forever. In the dark, a ray of light shone through the window.

Ken opened the door, and Suzuki entered. After speaking on the phone in Japanese, he covered the receiver to talk to me. "The hospital said your mom is still in a coma, but her condition is stabilized."

I fixed my eyes on him, yet looked past him. Mom laughed and sang in the yard of the house she and Dad built. "Sakura, Sakura..."

Ken gave my back a light pat. Then he shook hands with Suzuki. "Sorry to have bothered you so early in the morning."

"No problem. If I can do anything else, please let me know." Suzuki crossed to the door. "Ruth, don't worry about work. I'll tell Andrew about your situation."

***

At the airport, Cousin Albert held Jonny's duffle bag stuffed with clothes and books.

"Why can't I go with you? I won't cause any trouble. Please, take me with you." Jonny sobbed so hard that he hiccupped.

Agony seared my heart, and tears streamed down my cheeks.

Ken stooped to Jonny's level. "You can't skip school, right?"

Jonny wiped his face with his hand. "But I don't want to be here alone."

"You won't be alone. You'll stay with us." Ken's aunt patted Jonny's head. "Plus, you can play games with Doug every night. Don't you like playing with him?"

"Mommy, don't go." Jonny moved away from Ken and flung his arms around my waist.

I summoned a shaky smile and kissed his forehead. "Darling, Mommy has to go. Nana is sick. She needs me there."

He released his grip and walked to Ken. "Daddy, you stay."

Ken hugged him. "Son, Mommy can't handle this on her own. Be a good boy. We'll be back on Saturday. All will be well."

Jonny pulled his pouty face, his eyes welling up and his lower lip curling out. "Why can't I go with you?"

"We've talked about this," Ken whispered as he bent to Jonny's height again. "We love you very much and will see you in a few days."

Cousin Albert spoke aloud, "You'd better go. It'll take a while to go through the security checkpoint and customs."

Ken let go of Jonny and moved toward the Passenger Only sign. I gave my son one last kiss and quickened my steps to catch up with my husband. Behind me, Jonny's sobs turned into howling wails. I plugged my ears until I couldn't hear him anymore.

***

Three days after the call from Japan, Ken and I arrived in Tokyo. Heidi and Pastor Cheng from Mom's church picked us up from the airport and took us to the hospital.

Mom lay on her back with tubes all over her body. My stony façade shattered. I grasped her arm and screamed, "Mom, I'm here! Do you hear me?"

Her eyes were still closed, but her body jerked. The cardiac monitor by her bedside showed her heart beating faster. I thought she would wake up.

Yet no. She didn't.

Ken touched my back. "Speak in a calmer tone."

I heeded his command and stroked her cheek. "It's Mimi. I'm here for you. I love you very much."

Tears trickled down my face and dripped onto the bedsheet. She stopped moving, and her heartbeats returned to normal.

A nurse walked in and spoke in rapid Japanese. Pastor Cheng translated for us. "They need to move your mom to another room for an examination. We must leave."

He and Heidi brought us to the Metropolitan Hotel in Ikebukuro. "Our church isn't far from here. My family lives in the parsonage. If you need anything, call me, and I can be here in five minutes."

While I kept quiet, Ken shook hands with him. "Pastor Cheng, thank you so much."

His lips curled into a grin. "We are brothers and sisters in Christ. I'm sure you'd do the same for me."

After they left, Ken approached me. "Should we pray?"

I shook my head. I had nothing to say to God.

Ken sighed and prayed by himself. "Lord, please help us face this circumstance with courage and wisdom. I ask for Your protection over Mom. Life is in Your hands. If You want her to be with You, please let her leave in peace and with dignity—"

I bolted upright and hit my husband's arm with my fist. "How could you say that? No. She has to recover. I won't let her..."

I broke down and howled.

"Oh, Ruth." His voice sounded distant.

I buried my face in his shoulder. Memories of Dad's passing crashed into me. I shivered. "I'm so scared."

"I know. I understand." He rubbed my back. "I'm sorry."

Night fell. Light filtered down in long shards from the lampshade. I leaned against Ken and wouldn't let him go. An unwelcome silence lurked. My stomach rumbled.

Ken touched my hair. "We haven't eaten anything since we arrived. Let me go buy dinner for us. We need to take good care of ourselves in order to help Mom."

Somehow, I loosened my hold on his waist. After he left, I took out my cell phone and jotted down a few words in my diary. "I'm so fearful. Lord, please let my mom live."

I paused before typing again. "All along, I consider myself an independent, capable career woman. Sometimes, I even think I'm tougher than Ken. No. I'm still that sixteen-year-old helpless girl. My husband is the strong one. He understood my predicament, flew to Japan with me, and prayed for me."

Why did I give him such a harsh response when he showed only kindness? Tears wet my face again. "Lord, I don't know what to say anymore. I need Your mercy and grace."

Ken returned with two boxes of curry chicken over rice. "Lots of people. The Japanese love curry dishes."

I took a few bites and stopped.

His chopsticks hovered over his box, a piece of chicken dangling in them. "Not to your taste?"

I didn't answer, but moved away and slumped into bed.

The sounds from the bathroom reached my ears. Then Ken crawled in next to me and turned off the bedside lamp.

In the darkness, I listened to his snoring. A scene from my past surged into my mind. After Dad died, I feared losing Mom so much that if I heard her coughing, I would force her to go see a doctor.

A silent scream went off in my head. "Mom, please don't die."

I tossed and turned. A strange idea emerged in my mind. *Mom is the sole barrier that separates me from death. Her departure means I'm next.*

Fear grappled my whole person once more.

***

Early in the morning, Pastor Cheng accompanied us to the hospital. He translated the doctor's words. "The major blood vessels in your mother's brain are blocked. Too bad nobody came to her rescue when it happened. The stroke affected two-thirds of her brain."

As if someone dumped a bucket of icy water over my head, those words washed away my last glimmer of hope that Mom might wake up. Although the doctor said little, I didn't need to understand his words to know what his sympathetic eyes seemed to tell—"Prepare for the funeral."

I forced myself to hold back tears. Yet my face must have contorted into an awful mask because Ken wrapped his arm around my shoulder.

Footsteps sounded, and Uncle Pei, his wife, and his daughter, Yuko, walked in. Uncle Pei spoke to Pastor Cheng in Taiwanese. "Pastor, thank you for letting us know." Then he shifted to Mom's bed and called, "Toshiko."

Mom's body didn't stir.

After Pastor Cheng drew him and his family aside and explained Mom's condition, Uncle Pei spun toward me, his eyes moist. "Your mom is kind and brave. I'm sure she wants you to be courageous in this situation."

"Uncle..." My voice cracked. I burst into uncontrollable sobs.

Ken held me even tighter, and Uncle Pei stepped closer to embrace both of us.

A stillness fell over the room.

Amid the apprehensive quietness, someone coughed. The doctor said something. Pastor Cheng turned to Ken and me. "They'll do an MRI soon. The results will show whether your mom can breathe on her own. If she can't, they need to do a procedure called a tracheostomy. It's to create an opening at the front of her neck so a tube can be inserted into the windpipe to help her breathe."

Hadn't she suffered enough? A shiver ran up my spine.

A nurse entered, bowed to the doctor, and spoke in a soft tone. Pastor Cheng urged us to leave. "She's ready to take your mom to the MRI scanning center now."

Before Uncle Pei's family left, Yuko grasped my arm. "Has Auntie Su-Hua come to see your mom?"

My shoulders stiffened. "No."

"I've told her the hospital's name and address. She may stop by." She let go of my hand, then patted it. "Bye. Take care."

Pastor Cheng took us to his favorite place on a quiet street for lunch. "They have excellent Japanese ramen."

We stopped in front of a dingy little restaurant. Almost one in the afternoon, yet the place overflowed with patrons.

The noodles came. I sampled them and had to agree the ramen was outstanding. As always, good food brought me comfort and warmth. My trepidation eased a little.

After we returned to our hotel together, Pastor Cheng pulled out a chair. "Is it possible to change your flights?"

"I've been thinking about it as well." Ken blew out a heavy breath. "The uncertainties won't go away before Saturday."

Knowing my husband took his Sunday responsibilities seriously, I couldn't help chiming in. "What about your sermon?"

He glanced at his watch. "It's late in Chicago, but Pastor Rich is a night owl. Let me contact him. He can preach for me if someone does the translation into Chinese for him."

While Ken texted on the phone, I explained to Pastor Cheng. "Our church has three pastors. Ken mainly takes care of the Chinese congregation. Pastor Terri is for the English congregation. Pastor Rich is our youth pastor."

Ken returned to my side. "I've also sent Albert a message to tell him we can't make it back to Chicago this Saturday. Hope Jonny won't be too upset."

The corners of my eyes tightened. "I have to email my boss and coworkers to let them know I won't be at work until next week."

Pastor Cheng called United for us, and we changed our flights to next Thursday. Then he gestured for us to sit on the sofa. "One more thing I need to tell you. If your mom is still alive later this week, be prepared that the hospital will ask you to move her to a nursing facility."

I jolted my gaze up and gasped. The idea never crossed my mind. Ken inclined his head. "I used to work as a hospital chaplain. I'm familiar with the discharge process."

Pastor Cheng rubbed his forehead. "There are some differences in the healthcare systems between Japan and the US. Let's talk to the hospital tomorrow. Maybe they can help." He tapped his fingers on the side table. "By the way, after Saturday, you are more than welcome to stay in one of the classrooms in our church. You may have heard that houses in Tokyo are expensive and pitifully tiny. I'm sorry we don't have spare rooms in the parsonage for you, but you can come to my house to take showers."

Ken and I exchanged a glance.

Pastor Cheng continued. "Although your mom has insurance, the bill may shock you. Try to save money whenever and wherever you can."

Ken scratched his chin, one of his habits when he became emotional. "You hardly know us. How can we thank you for your kindness?"

Pastor Cheng grinned. "Like what I said before, I'm sure you'd do the same for me should I be in your position."

Chapter Nineteen

At the hospital the next morning, I massaged my forehead in a vain attempt to ease the pain thumping against my temples.

Ken touched my arm. "Do you have a headache? Didn't you sleep well last night?"

I ignored him and hurried toward Mom. She lay motionless like before. At least the machine indicated her heartbeat was steady.

The doctor entered with a few films. He gestured for us to gather around him and spoke to Pastor Cheng.

"Look at this." He showed the first picture. "All these are indications of vessel blockage." Flipping to another one, he added, "Same here. More than three-quarters of her brain has been affected."

Pastor Cheng's translation followed. "Even if she wakes up from her coma, she'll likely remain in a semi-vegetative state. She can't eat or breathe on her own."

Tears welled up in my eyes, and I shifted a few steps away from the doctor.

Ken tugged at my sleeve. "The doctor wants you to sign this."

I lifted my gaze. But before me stood my mother, a younger, happier version of Mom. She was singing her cherry blossom song in our yard, surrounded by white blossoms on the plum trees.

R. F. Whong

Someone waved in front of me and snapped me out of my thoughts. Pastor Cheng pointed at a blank space. "The hospital needs your approval for the tracheostomy procedure."

Ken gave me a pen, and I signed.

The doctor signaled for us to leave. Pastor Cheng explained. "They will perform the procedure soon. We can come back this afternoon."

With reluctance, I followed the others into the hallway.

A familiar voice asked, "Are you Mimi?"

I shuffled back a step. *Except for Mom, who else would call me Mimi?*

I gawked at the battered and old woman.

"I'm your aunt Su-Hua." A grin diffused across her wrinkled face.

Life hadn't been kind to her. I shifted my gaze away. She used to be young and beautiful. Now she looked like a wilted flower.

When did I last see her? Almost thirty years ago.

Ken extended his hand to her. "Auntie Su-Hua, I'm Ken, Ruth's husband."

"Yeah, I recognize you. My sister-in-law showed me your pictures all the time. She's very fond of you." Auntie Su-Hua pulled me into a hug. "Mimi, you're all grown up, but your appearance hasn't changed much."

I clenched my teeth against the pain inside of me. A tangled mess of emotions boiled up. Confusion? Anger? Sadness?

Auntie Su-Hua hung her arm around me. "Yuko called me this morning, and I came right away. How is your mom?"

Liar. Yuko called you yesterday.

"Thank you so much for coming." Ken cast me a wary glance. "Although her condition is stable, Mom still hasn't come out of the coma."

Su-Hua dragged her hands down the sides of her face. "How awful. Why is everyone sick? Earlier this year, your uncle Pei had a heart attack. Now, it's your mom. Maybe I'll be the next."

Passing by the nurse's station, Pastor Cheng stopped to speak to the girl on duty, then said to us, "I asked if we could return to your mom's room to let your aunt see her. But she said no."

Su-Hua covered her nose with a handkerchief. "It's okay. I can come again tomorrow." She took two steps toward me, covering the

145

distance between us. "Your mom bought a new refrigerator and a washing machine recently. Can I have them? Also, if you don't need her bed and table, I'll take them as well."

Shock blasted through me. "What?" I slapped a palm over my mouth, too late to mute my shout.

The young nurse left her station and said something. Her scowl brought heat to my cheeks.

"Sorry." Ken apologized on my behalf, then faced Auntie Su-Hua. "We haven't had a chance to visit Mom's unit in the retirement home yet. We'll call you later."

Auntie Su-Hua bobbed her head and trod away.

Pastor Cheng soon left as well. With only Ken around, my pent-up irritation broke free. "How could Auntie Su-Hua say that? She hasn't changed a bit. It's always me, me, me. Does she have any concern for Mom's welfare?"

Ken grasped my arm. "Ruth, Auntie Su-Hua doesn't know God. Most people who have no God in their lives are self-centered."

I continued to rant, my hands fisting, my fingernails biting into my palms. "She always puts her interests first. She's never satisfied."

"She's also miserable, unhappy. Didn't you tell me she isn't sixty? She looks so much older than her age." He halted and gripped my arm, then slid his hand down to loosen my fist. "Pray about it. Think about what Mom would do under this circumstance. Would she gladly give Su-Hua the appliances she no longer needs?"

His words hit me hard. *The appliances she no longer needs.*

Tears stung my eyelids. "You don't think Mom will come out of the coma?"

He averted his gaze.

It would take a miracle for her to regain consciousness. "Can we pray for her to wake up? Maybe God will give us a miracle."

Ken hesitated. I detected the thoughts flashing through his mind because we'd discussed Jesus' miracles not long ago. His words still resonated with me. "From my studies of the Bible, a specific purpose stood behind every one of Jesus' miracles."

Lord, should I seek a miracle for my mother?

"You can ask God for His mercy on you and Mom." Ken's tone was more gentle than usual.

"I want her to be around as long as possible—no matter what."

Why did I say that? A shiver rippled through me. Would Mom consider God's mercy in a different light?

We entered our room, and I dragged my exhausted body to bed. Yet my brain had other ideas. I stared at the ceiling and let time pass by me.

The door opened, then clicked shut again. Ken must have left. I got up. The clock on the wall indicated twelve twenty.

I typed into the diary on my cell phone. "How do we define life? Can someone unconscious or in a semi-vegetative state be considered a person?"

Not finding any immediate answer, I threw the phone into my purse. Ken's Bible on the coffee table caught my attention. During the past years, I'd switched to an electronic Bible on my phone. I'd even told Ken with pride, "This way, I can read different versions easily."

Yet now, holding a physical book in hand brought me a solid awareness of God's presence. I flipped to Psalm 139, pausing at two familiar verses. "My frame was not hidden from you when I was made in the secret place. When I was woven together in the depths of the earth, your eyes saw my unformed body."

If God saw an unformed baby, of course, God knew Mom in her state. To Him, she remained a complete, valuable person.

Love and peace flowed through me like a gentle stream. *Lord, thank You for Your words.*

The lock turned, and Ken strolled in with two lunch boxes. His eyes stretched wide when I grinned. "The first smile since we got Heidi's call. What's going on?"

"I received the assurance from God that He is still with us." I drew him to the sofa. "No matter what happens next, God loves Mom."

"I'm glad to hear that." He brushed my bangs aside and kissed my forehead, then drew me back to arm's length. "Watch out for a fluctuation of emotions in the next few days as the situation changes."

I gave him a hard stare. "You talk like a therapist."

He cuffed my shoulder. "I'm a pastor trained in professional counseling."

Warmth crept into my heart as he tried to make this light moment last. "What did you get? Curry chicken again?"

"Something you like. Ramen with seafood." He placed a box before me. "Let's eat. We'll go to the hospital with Pastor Cheng at three."

Back in the Intensive Care Unit, I examined the tube inserted into the hole at the front of Mom's neck. My own throat closed, and I struggled to swallow the rush of saliva in my mouth. "Does it hurt?"

Her body stirred at my murmur. Ken hugged my shoulders from behind. I turned and buried my face in the crook of his neck.

"They had to do it." Pastor Cheng came forward. "It's a step toward getting her out of the ICU."

I shifted away from Ken. "She's still unconscious."

"That doesn't affect their decision." Pastor Cheng released a deep breath. "Many stroke or heart attack patients never regain consciousness. As soon as their conditions stabilize, the hospital moves them into nursing facilities."

An image of Nancy's roommate, along with her breathing machine and feeding tube, came to mind. The last time when Ken and I visited Nancy in the nursing home, Joseph whispered to us, "That poor woman has been in a vegetative state for over five years. A victim of a massive heart attack."

I drew my brows tight. Why couldn't my extensive scientific training help my own mother? No, not even one bit.

Pastor Cheng checked his watch. "Your mom's retirement home called me earlier. They want you to close her account."

I jerked my head up. "Why?"

He scratched his chin. "The center only accepts seniors who can take care of themselves. There's a long waiting list."

"But..."

Ken coughed and interrupted me. "I understand. Could you please go with us?"

"Sure. Few Japanese people speak English."

Shortly later, I trekked behind Ken and Pastor Cheng to step into the tiny garden leading to the building. At the sight of the Japanese maple tree, moisture gathered behind my eyelids.

Last time I saw you, your gorgeous red leaves were on full display.

Now, bare branches showed no sign of life.

I stilled my steps. Mom's Taiwanese rang in my ears. "What do you want for dinner? Beef? Fish? Or chicken?"

How long ago? Was it when Ken started serving at our first church?

After Mom learned I struggled to fit into my role as a pastor's wife, she invited me to see her in Tokyo. We took a wonderful trip together, all the way to Hokkaidō.

Then we had Jonny, and she formed the habit of visiting us every year.

I paced underneath the tree, waiting for Ken and Pastor Cheng to get a key from the office. Perspiration wetted my palms.

I hadn't seen her room in such a long time. What would I discover?

The two men reappeared. Pastor Cheng excused himself and took leave, and I dragged my legs to follow Ken through the door.

A picture of a gorgeous woman hung on the wall. Jade bangles dangled on her wrist. Yeah, the enlarged duplicate of the only remaining picture of Mom's mother, my grandma, who died young.

Her beautiful eyes followed me as I surveyed the unit. The refrigerator looked new. I opened the door. Nothing was in it except a head of lettuce and a half-eaten piece of cake.

A box of instant noodles lay on top of the fridge. I blinked and attempted to make sense of the scene.

Lettuce, cake, and instant noodles? Were those what she ate day after day? Where were the beef, fish, and chicken?

Next to the fridge sat a table with two chairs. Four bowls, five spoons, and three pairs of chopsticks lay in a neat array on a stand.

Memories of our numerous arguments over how she'd hand-washed dishes crashed over me. Why did I squabble with her all the time?

Ken's voice sounded from the bathroom, interrupting my thoughts. "The washing machine does look new."

I ignored him and entered the bedroom. The room, bare like the other one, showed a full-size bed, a nightstand, and a plastic closet against one wall.

Did her place look so desolate when I last visited her?

Didn't we sleep together here? Why didn't I feel anything amiss back then?

"Because she was here." I whispered the answer as it came to me. Her laughter lilted through the air with wings, filling every corner.

I sat on the bed, and my gaze drifted toward the worn book on the nightstand—the Chinese Bible I gave her as her baptism gift years ago.

Her testimony on that day remained vivid. "I chose Naomi as my baptismal name because my life is a testimony that God can change 'Mara' into 'Naomi.'"

A piece of paper in the corner caught my attention. I picked it up and touched Mom's handwriting. "Remember to buy Su-Hua a box of mochi."

A reminder note to herself.

Mom's words echoed in my head. "Su-Hua's son loves mochi."

Ken stepped in. "Did you say something?"

I shook my head hard.

He opened the closet door. The answering machine I gave her some time ago lay at the bottom. "Pastor Cheng wanted us to find Mom's checkbook."

Yeah, Mom still lived in the twentieth century.

"She has the habit of storing her valuables in her clothes." I helped him find a long coat.

He scrutinized it. "Looks like the one she picked up from the Salvation Army a few years back when she visited us."

My lips curled into a half smile. "She's never worn it. Its entire purpose is for storage."

We located a booklet from her bank in one of its pockets.

I grabbed another jacket and found a seal.

"Great." Ken took it from me. "Pastor Cheng said in Japan a name seal is required to withdraw money."

I flipped through her bank records. "Mom gets ninety-eight thousand yen each month from the government."

The last entry was a number: 1,100,900.

Was that all she had? Not even nine thousand US dollars.

The camel-hair coat, the cashmere sweater, and the silk dress she gave us last April... Was that why she skimped on food?

She saved money to buy expensive gifts for us and Auntie Su-Hua.

Tears stung my cheeks.

"I know your thoughts. Mom is the opposite of Auntie Su-Hua." Ken dabbed my face with a Kleenex, then hugged me. "Speaking of Su-Hua, should I call her and ask her to come tomorrow? She'll need help to move the heavy items. Pastor Cheng mentioned some young men from his church can help."

As I hid my face in his chest, Ken murmured, "Su-Hua is doing us a great favor. Otherwise, we must pay someone to clean out Mom's unit."

Chapter Twenty

After we followed Pastor Cheng into the hallway leading to Mom's room, a uniformed nurse approached us. Unlike the other nurses with their soft voices, she stretched out her arm and spoke in a strong, modulated tone. Pastor Cheng translated for us. "Your mom is no longer in 3N. They've transferred her into 2N."

I jerked my gaze up. "Mom is out of the ICU?"

Pastor Cheng repeated my question in Japanese. The woman replied with a nod.

I shifted one step toward her and asked in English, "Has my mom come out of her coma?"

Her face clouded, and she held both hands, palms upward. After Pastor Cheng talked to her, she shook her head and excused herself.

I dragged my sneaker across the floor, tracing the line of the linoleum. "Why did they move Mom from the ICU to the ward if she's still in the coma?"

Ken gave my shoulder a gentle pat. "Mom's condition must have stabilized to a point that she doesn't need intensive care anymore."

Pastor Cheng drew his thick eyebrows tight. "It may also mean the hospital expects us to find a nursing facility in the next few days."

"How do we do it?" Ken touched his chin, a nervous habit of his.

"We'll need to discuss it with the doctor." Pastor Cheng compressed his mouth.

I edged away, uncertain whether to see Mom or find the doctor first.

Ken made it easy for me. "Let's go to Room 2N, then talk to the doctor."

Mom lay alone in her room. The EEG monitor and other machines were gone, but she was still tethered to her feeding tube and breathing machine. The hiss of the ventilator broke the heavy stillness.

I scudded over to her bedside. "It's Mimi here."

My eyes caught something unusual. She dipped her chin, a movement indistinct but certain.

I shouted at Ken. "Mom nodded."

He hurried to my side. "Are you sure?"

"Yes." I bent over Mom. "It's Mimi. Do you hear me?"

This time, she bobbed her head twice. One of her eyelids twitched. I picked up her hand. "Are you trying to open your eyes?"

A faint moan escaped her mouth. Pastor Cheng came over. "She may come around."

I hugged her body. "Mom, I need you. Please wake up."

Both of her eyelids twitched. I held my breath. Then her face returned to motionless. Without the cardiac monitor, the only indication that eased my dread came from the almost imperceptible rise and fall of the sheet over her chest.

Moisture dampened my cheeks. I released my hold on her. "She isn't waking up."

Ken cradled me into an embrace. "Oh, Ruth."

"The doctor is here," Pastor Cheng called out.

I spun toward him. "Pastor Cheng, please tell the doctor what we've seen."

The doctor pressed his lips together while listening.

I rubbed my forehead. "He doesn't believe us?"

"No." Pastor Cheng cleared his throat.

Mom's eyelids fluttered, and her right arm jiggled.

I shrieked. "Something is happening."

While all of us stared at Mom's face, she opened her eyes, then squeezed them shut again as if the lights were too bright.

I lifted a simple prayer, thanking the Lord, and grasped Mom's hand. "I love you very much."

A single drop of tear slid down her cheek. Her fingers coiled around mine.

"It's okay." I wiped away the moisture for her. "It'll be all right."

In English, I asked the doctor, "My mom opened her eyes. Do you think she's regained consciousness?"

He seemed caught off guard, then launched into a lengthy speech in Japanese.

Pastor Cheng stepped in. "He said sometimes people in a coma may open and close their eyes because of involuntary movements. He doubts how much brain function she still has."

So, the doctor understood English. I pressed on. "My mom shed a tear after I told her I loved her."

The doctor replied in Japanese, his tone deliberate and serious.

"He still doesn't think your mom has snapped out of her coma. Even if she did, her brain function is minimal." Pastor Cheng gestured for Ken and me to move near him. "The doctor also said they've contacted several nursing facilities in their system. None has agreed to take her."

I raised my eyebrows. "Why?"

Pastor Cheng scratched his ear. "In Japan, the patient's family is responsible for all the daily necessities, such as diapers, towels, and clothing. Since your mom has no family in Tokyo, they..." He shrugged.

My heart sank, and I exchanged a glance with Ken. Why was Japan's healthcare system so complicated? "What else can we do?"

Ken touched his chin. "Is there any alternative?"

When the doctor mumbled something and took leave, Pastor Cheng crossed his arms over his chest and shifted his feet. "Dennis may be able to help."

"Dennis? Heidi's husband?" I bit my lip.

"He runs a dialysis center and has patients from different assisted living facilities. He has close ties with many of them." Pastor Cheng took out his cell phone. "Let me ask him."

While he spoke in Japanese, I stood rooted to the ground, weighed down by the stiffness of my shoulders and the sweat on my neck.

At last, he put his phone away. "Dennis said he would make a few calls. He sounded quite positive."

I pressed him. "When can we get an answer?"

My husband tugged at my sleeve. "I'm sure Dennis will try his best. Let's pray about it. God willing, we may get some positive news later today."

"Well said." Pastor Cheng nodded. "Let's get back to your hotel. You can check out and move your luggage to our church."

Already Saturday? Did Auntie Su-Hua help clean out Mom's room yesterday? No, that was two nights ago.

Before we left, I sat by Mom and ran my fingers through her hair. "I'm leaving now, but will be back this afternoon."

She didn't stir.

Ken stood behind me. "She's probably asleep."

As we dragged our Pullman suitcases across the uneven sidewalks in Ikebukuro, light snow began falling.

Pastor Cheng pulled his scarf up to cover his nose and mouth. "Miserable weather. And what terrible timing."

Ken's lips curved up into a half smile. "This is nothing in Chicago."

"Ah, I forgot you two are from the Windy City." Pastor Cheng stopped in front of a skyscraper and retrieved an item from his pocket. "A spare key for you. Try it. Make sure you can unlock the door."

A small cross hung a few feet above the door.

Ken got it open at his first attempt, and we hurried inside.

"Our church occupies three stories here. The sanctuary is on the first floor. Sunday school rooms are on the second, and offices on the third."

"Who owns the other stories?" I asked.

"Different organizations, including some for-profit companies." Pastor Cheng led us to the sanctuary. "I'm thankful the property owner, a Taiwanese Christian, donated the space to the church."

Ken surveyed the stage. "How many members do you have?"

"About a hundred. Churches in Japan are small, especially ours, an ethnic church. Unlike in the States, few churches in Tokyo can afford to have a stand-alone building." Pastor Cheng directed us out of the worship hall. "How about yours?"

"We have about four hundred." Ken gave the area one last glance. "Have you been to the States?"

"I've visited California. I'm envious that most of the Chinese churches there have large parking lots surrounding the stand-alone properties." Pastor Cheng led the way toward the staircase. "Parking is a problem in Tokyo. But public transportation is cheap and convenient."

"I heard it's tough to preach the gospel here." Ken quickened his steps to catch up. "I wonder why."

"Very difficult." Pastor Cheng's lips sagged at the corners. "Many factors to consider. Japanese people value conformity. The society expects you to look and act like everyone else. In addition, a certain code of perfectionism is at play. That's why Japan makes high-quality cars and electronics. The culture doesn't like the idea of sin, which is equivalent to imperfection. When we share the gospel, we have to tell someone he's a sinner and needs salvation from Jesus. Those words aren't easily accepted here."

The two men lapsed into silence up the stairs.

I followed them. "Where is your parsonage?"

"In an apartment nearby." Pastor Cheng helped us settle into one of the classrooms. "Call me if you need anything."

After Pastor Cheng left, I dropped my suitcase and inched toward Ken. "Do you think Mom has come out of her coma? Or was the doctor right?"

Ken stopped unpacking. "I'm not sure."

I burst out crying, releasing all my pent-up emotions. "But Mom's fingers wrapped around mine when I held her hand."

His shoulders curled forward, another habit of his that I knew too well. He dreaded saying words that might hurt others. "Let's take it one day at a time."

I slouched forward and buried my face in my lap. "Mom must come out of her coma. She can't leave me like this."

He drew me to his bosom. "Learn not to hold on to things so tight. Otherwise, it hurts when God pries your fingers open to take them away."

A fire ignited in me. "Don't preach."

He lapsed into silence and held me more tightly.

I sobbed into his shirt. Somehow, my eyelids grew heavy. I hadn't slept well since my arrival. A nap might relieve me from this nightmare.

Yet sleep still eluded me. My brain raced in search of a solution. "Maybe we should consider moving Mom back to the States."

Ken rubbed my back. "I thought about it when we first arrived. I did some online research. It's difficult, almost impossible. The airline needs assurance that the patient is well enough to fly. Otherwise, they encounter liability issues. A medical doctor specializing in emergency care has to accompany her in case something happens."

I raised my gaze. "Is there any way out?"

His hand stilled on my waist. "Think about what Mom would have wanted. Would she prefer to stay in Tokyo, a place she feels more at ease? Or would she like to be moved to a location where people speak English?"

My conversation with Mom in the Chicago Botanic Garden swept across my mind. "Mom told me I should cremate her body after she died and spread the ashes into the Pacific Ocean. What went through her mind when she said that? Japan or the US? The Pacific Ocean connects both countries."

Ken loosened his hold of me. "Does Mom have an advance directive, a document that specifies what she wants?"

I wiped tears away, lifted my chin, and brushed my bangs back into place. "Did you mean a living will? For someone like Mom who doesn't use a cell phone? I don't think so. We haven't even set our own up."

A haunted look shadowed Ken's eyes as if he got sucked into a sudden storm. "As soon as we get back to the States, we'll need to put together a will, a health directive, and a living trust. Jonny is still young. We must make sure things are in order should something happen to us."

A pang shot through me. "Jonny cried so hard when I called him yesterday. He wanted my promise we'll be home next Thursday."

I heaved out a heavy breath, but couldn't lift the feelings of misery.

Ken coiled his fingers into a tight ball. "Let's take one step at a time. First, we need to ensure Mom has a nursing placement."

I massaged my temple. Ken was right. What was becoming of me? Where did my analytical skills go? "Should we call Dennis?"

He shook his head. "Today is Saturday. We probably won't get an answer until Monday morning. Dennis will call us when he—"

The phone rang.

"Hello?" He took a step away from me. "Hi, Dennis."

As he listened, a smile spread out on his lips. "I'll tell her. We'll go over immediately."

I staggered toward Ken after he hung up. "Has Dennis found a place for Mom?"

He murmured, "Praise the Lord."

Someone knocked. Then Pastor Cheng walked in. "Has Dennis called you?"

Ken nodded. "I didn't expect it to happen so fast."

Pastor Cheng chuckled, his excitement contagious. "I told you Dennis knows those people well." His chin dropped. "Did he tell you the conditions?"

What conditions? I glared at Ken.

"He did." Ken patted my arm. "Sorry, I haven't had a chance to tell you."

Pastor Cheng shifted his weight from one foot to the other. "The up-front fee is substantial. I've converted it into US dollars. It's fifty thousand to get in, then a hundred and eighty-five a day."

"Dennis is very kind. Since Ruth's mom doesn't have enough money in her account, he'll pay the difference for now. Once we get back to the States, we'll wire him the money." Ken kneaded his brows. "I'm more concerned about the requirement. They want us to sign an agreement to guarantee someone will bring them the supplies every Monday. How are we going to do that?"

"Our church can help." Pastor Cheng waved a hand. "We'll form a rotating team of four, so each person only has to do it once a month. When there's a fifth week, I'll fill in."

Moisture stung my eyelids once more. "Sorry to cause so much trouble."

"As brothers and sisters in God's family, we ought to take care of each other." Pastor Cheng glanced at his watch. "We'd better go. Dennis said he'll meet us at Marumo Hospital."

"Marumo Hospital?" I blurted out. "I thought it was a nursing home."

"Well, in Japan, we call nursing homes hospitals." Pastor Cheng led the way out.

Chapter Twenty-One

The elevator climbed to the fourth floor. Anxiety overwhelmed me, and my toes tingled inside my shoes.

Lord, I pray for no complications during Mom's transport to Marumo Hospital.

The door opened, and I followed my companions out.

We walked down the corridor to enter Room 2N. Mom's eyes were closed.

Good. She wouldn't have to suffer the jolts and jerks of the ride.

I inspected the surroundings, then spoke to Ken in a low voice. "Looks like everything is in order."

Before he responded, Pastor Cheng patted Ken's arm. "The ambulance only allows two of the patient's family members. Dennis suggested you and I take a taxi and let him and Ruth go with her mom."

A nurse walked in and uttered something to Dennis in Japanese.

He shifted to Mom's bed. "The ambulance is here. Let's go."

As paramedics loaded Mom up into the ambulance, a shudder ran up my spine. The question I entered in my diary earlier popped up again. *How does one define life?*

I shook my head hard and crawled in with the others. *Try to concentrate. It's not the right time to think about philosophy.*

While the siren sounded and the van zigzagged through Tokyo's busy streets, Dennis engaged in a conversation with the doctor who accompanied us. Their incomprehensible phrases flew over me and vanished into space.

I grasped Mom's fingers. No response.

Mom's retirement home bedroom... Did I get her Bible last week? Where did I put it?

Not even a few days had passed. Why did it feel like a long time ago?

An even more distant scene crossed my mind.

Was I six or seven? The morning sun filtered through the windowpane and warmed my cheeks. I pressed my face against Mom's lap and demanded, "Clean my ears, please."

She touched my hair, her laughter lilting through the air. "Not again. Didn't we do it yesterday?"

"It didn't count," I grumbled.

She got a cotton swab and gave my ear canal a light jab. "Okay. Done."

"No." I twisted my body. "One more, please."

Fingers wrapped around my hand, I jolted my head up, tender memories fleeting away. "Mom, are you awake?"

She gave a slight nod.

No matter what others say, I believe she's come out of her coma.

Yet I couldn't gauge how much brain function she still had.

I leaned forward and whispered, "Remember you used to clean my ears? From day one, your care nourished me. After Dad passed away, your encouragements and reprimands guided me through those difficult days. I've always benefited from your selfless love. Mom, you're a wonderful mother."

Her eyes fluttered open. I gazed at her and read her expressions under the veil of illness. Her concerns and questions became visible, like fish swimming at the bottom of a clear stream. Rampant words tumbled out of my mouth. "Ken and I have everything under control. Jonny is staying with Ken's aunt and his cousin Doug. Auntie Su-Hua was so kind to help us clean out your apartment last week. We've closed your account with the retirement home."

Remorse swept across my soul at my realization of my white lies, yet I kept going. "Uncle Pei and Auntie Su-Hua came to the hospital to see you many times. Yesterday, Auntie Su-Hua even treated us to a wonderful dinner."

I paused. My thoughts turned to our *sashimi* dinner with Auntie Su-Hua last night. Ken didn't eat raw fish.

Mom blinked twice as if encouraging me to say more.

"Oh yes. We're on our way to Marumo Hospital. They provide excellent care for people like you. They'll put you into their rehabilitation program." I gave her hand a gentle squeeze. "Don't be anxious about the expenses. It's quite affordable."

Another pang of guilt stabbed my conscience. I swallowed hard to keep it down. "Don't worry about my job. I have enough vacation days, and we're heading back home the day after tomorrow."

An indescribable sound, like a moan or a gasp, escaped Mom's mouth. Her eyes became moist. Soon, tears trickled down her cheeks. Did the mention of my leaving upset her? Did she understand what I said?

I wiped her face clean, then stroked her forehead. "You won't be here alone. The Lord is with you. Plus, Pastor Cheng has mobilized the whole church to take care of you. And Ken and I will come to see you again as often as we can."

Someone tapped my shoulder. My arm jerked, and Mom's fingers slipped out of mine. The van jolted and stopped. Dennis stood up. "We are here."

***

On the day of our departure, before we left for the airport, I sat by Mom's bed and clipped her nails. Her eyes fixed on me, her pupils enlarged.

Was she trying to tell me something?

Yet this time, I couldn't decipher her feelings. I dropped the nail clipper into my purse. Her right hand inched toward mine. I grasped it and brought it to my lips. "Mom, I love you very much."

Moisture shimmered in her eyes. I hugged her, letting my own tears flow into her gown. "I'll come again soon."

Why did separation bring such intense agony? The pain I'd experienced from Jonny's wail at O'Hare last week paled in comparison.

On the plane, I kept weeping. Ken gave my arm a gentle pat. "Try to take a nap. You'll need to go to work after we get back."

I squeezed my eyelids shut in a vain attempt to bring on some sleep. The past ten days replayed in my head—Mom in the hospital, her apartment with meager food in the fridge, my messy emotions when I ran into Auntie Su-Hua....

The cabin lights dimmed, and Ken dozed off. I jammed my knees into the seat in front and prayed. *Lord, why is life so difficult? What'll happen next?*

Amid my tumultuous thoughts, a hymn emerged—"I Know Who Holds Tomorrow."

Oh, Lord, is it a reminder that You're still in control? Will my mom recover?

The plane made a soft, smooth landing. I twisted my watch into view. A few minutes before noon. Should I go to the office?

Ken looked out the window. "We'll have to hail a taxi. I asked Albert not to come to the airport. Today is his workday."

"Jonny won't be out of school until three. We've got time." I covered a yawn.

He tucked me under his arm. "Yeah, I'll go to my aunt's house to pick him up. Are you going to work?"

My hazy head tallied my remaining vacation days. "I'd better go in."

Two hours later, I dragged my sleep-deprived body down the staircase at work and peeked into Andrew's office. He jerked his gaze up. "You're back. Come on in."

The ice in his tone jolted me awake and caused my heart to lurch. With a robotic movement, I pulled out a chair to sit down.

Andrew tapped the desk with his fingers. "The performance review is coming up in less than three months. Remember, you can't wait until the last minute to tell your subordinate he doesn't perform. Have you talked to Suzuki about his poor performance?"

The threat in his expression brought another shiver to my spine. I examined my hands, then returned my attention to him. "Suzuki's performance is excellent like before. He received outstanding ratings in the past. If I give him a poor rating this year, how do I justify it to him and my previous boss?"

Andrew's fingers stopped tapping, their stillness almost more annoying than their rhythm had been. "I have a meeting with the vice president in five minutes. I'm sure you can come up with some good justifications. I'll check with you again next week." He stood up, a clear signal to dismiss me.

Okay, I got the message.

While passing through the long corridor, I looked out the window.

When did it start to snow?

I slowed my steps and watched naughty white flakes dance up and down. The entire world felt relaxed, yet my mind raced through different scenarios.

Before Mom suffered the stroke, hadn't I decided to follow Christ, even to the point of giving up my beloved biochemistry?

Life dealt me a wild card.

If Andrew fired me, what would I do?

A thin layer of fluffy snow lay on the ground. Blanketed in white, everything appeared tranquil.

Andrew was right. Suzuki's communication skill was poor.

But how could I use that as my justification? From the beginning, Suzuki's English was always laced with a heavy Japanese accent.

I swallowed hard and strolled to my lab.

Suzuki came forward. "I thought you wouldn't come to work today. How is your mom? Is she better?"

Warmth crept into my heart. Suzuki cared about me, and Andrew had no compassion at all. "I believe she's out of her coma, although the doctors think her stroke has destroyed much of her brain function." I changed the subject. "How are things? Anything unusual?"

He didn't reply right away. After crossing to the door, he looked out into the hall, then came back and leaned against the epoxy resin bench. The tabletop centrifuge loomed over him. "Do you remember Glenn, who left the company last year?"

I slammed my body on the adjustable stool in front of me. "The Jewish guy with a kippah on his head? Of course. I took over his position. What about him?"

Suzuki crooked up a corner of his mouth into a peculiar smile. "I heard a rumor. When Glenn left, he filed a complaint to HR about Andrew's misconduct. At that time, Peter suppressed the case."

I shrugged and grabbed a piece of kimwipe from the bench. Andrew and our big boss, Peter, were buddies. The two frequented the bar together at least once a week.

Why would Suzuki bring this up?

He shifted his feet and adjusted his eyeglasses. "Glenn's complaints have resurfaced. I got insider information. Peter is leaving."

"Really?" My heart skipped a beat. "Impossible! He's been with the company for years." I lifted my head, then lowered it again.

Even if Peter was gone, Andrew had a knack for connecting with his new boss. All it took was one or two ball games together and a few drinks in the same bar. No doubt white males still dominated top management positions in most companies.

I massaged my temples, a useless attempt to ease the throbbing headache.

"Ruth, you don't look well. You should go home and rest." Suzuki stepped closer, frowning down at me. "Everything is in good order in the lab. Don't worry."

"Thank you." I brought a hand to my chest.

How many emails would be there for me to go through? Should I bring my laptop with me? Maybe not.

I crossed to my office and listened to the messages on the answering machine. Nothing grabbed my attention except one from Dr. Nelson. He asked to confirm the date of my seminar at his department early in March. I'd call him tomorrow and tell him I couldn't make it because of a family emergency.

Plopping down into my office chair, I turned on my computer and plowed through page after page of unread emails.

***

As soon as I entered our living room, Jonny rushed to me and wrapped his arms around my waist. "Mommy, Mommy."

"Son." Choked with emotions, I ran my fingers through his hair, and my sorrow mingled with guilt. "You look good."

I stooped to kiss his forehead. "Did you have a wonderful time playing with Doug?"

He pulled me toward the kitchen. "We played computer games every evening." As if remembering our family rules, he flashed a sheepish grin. "Well, only for a few minutes."

Seeing me, Ken set down the pan in his hand. "I cooked spaghetti and meatballs for tonight."

Tender feelings surged through me. My husband was so considerate.

Following dinner, Jonny scooted away to finish his homework. Ken and I remained at the table to chitchat as usual.

I kneaded my brows. "Andrew asked me about Suzuki's performance review again."

Ken gazed into my eyes. "Have you changed your mind about your decision?"

"If I stick to my principles, Andrew will fire me. What're we going to do then? Mom's nursing home costs almost two hundred a day. I can't afford to lose my job."

"Will you give in because you're concerned about money?" He scratched his chin. "Our motto is to honor God in whatever we do. It isn't easy, but God will give you courage and wisdom when you honor Him."

I bit the inside of my cheek. How could he view things so simply? "But how?"

The phone rang. Ken put it on speaker mode. "It's Pastor Cheng."

Pastor Cheng's booming voice filled the room. "I'm here with your mom. Her eyes are wide open as if searching for you. Do you want to speak to her?"

I grabbed the phone and cried out, tears welling up. "Ken and I are back at home safely. Don't worry about us. We'll come see you soon. Mom, I love you—" My throat closed up, and I halted.

My husband patted my arm. "Pastor Cheng, please tell her Ruth will see her in fourteen days. Sorry I don't speak Japanese or Taiwanese."

After our friend hung up, Ken handed me a piece of Kleenex. "United had a special fare from Chicago to Tokyo. I went ahead and booked one flight for you two weeks from now and another for me in about one month."

I parted my lips, forgetting to wipe my eyes. I used to be the one making all our travel arrangements. Out of his love for me, Ken did what he usually wouldn't do.

He returned to our dining table. "Your trip will be from Thursday to Monday to minimize the use of your vacation days, while mine will be from Monday to Friday, so I don't need to invite a guest speaker to give the sermon."

My jaw dropped further as I followed him to my chair. He thought of all the details.

"By the way"—he leaned in and touched my arm—"I know you haven't given up your idea of moving Mom to the States. I called Dr. Stone and told her about Mom's condition. I asked her whether it's okay for her to fly."

He hitched a breath. "Dr. Stone said not to transport her yet. We'll have to wait until she doesn't need the breathing machine. Plus, she cautioned me that Mom has no insurance in the US."

Raw emotions rushed to the surface, and my tears gushed out. "You don't want her here? If she were your mother, would you say the same?"

I sobbed so hard that my breath came in short gasps. Ken shifted to my side and wrapped his arms around me.

I slumped against him and wailed. "Why is life so difficult?"

He didn't respond, but hugged me tightly.

Unstoppable laments tumbled out of my mouth. "Mom lost her mother when she was a baby. Her stepmother abused her. Dad treated her well, but he died so young. I argue with her all the time. Now, this. Why does she endure so much suffering?"

Ken murmured, "Amid all the hardship, she's full of courage, grace, and love. I'm sure she wants you to be like her."

His words pierced my heart. "I'm not like her. I'm a mess."

He picked up my right hand and rubbed his thumb across my palm. "Remember how God helped you solve your tendon problems? Along the difficult path, He also reminded us of His amazing guidance through previous impossible challenges. God is still here with you today."

God is still here with you. The sentence echoed in my head.

Jonny walked in. My expression must have alarmed him, for he hurried to my side. "Mommy, are you all right?"

I wiped my face and forced a smile. "Mommy is okay. I just worry about Nana."

He stretched his arms wide open in an attempt to embrace both of us. "Mommy, don't cry. Let's pray for Nana and ask Jesus to heal her." He shut his eyes and lifted a prayer, pleading for God's protection over his nana.

I shifted my body and drew him into our three-way hug. If only I had faith like Jonny's.

Ken joined in and prayed, "Lord, I know Mom is Your beloved daughter. We love her, but You love her even more. No one can change that fact, not even illness."

He paused, waiting for me to carry on. I coughed and composed myself. "Dear heavenly Father, please have mercy on Mom. I am so weak and at a loss for what to do. Please give me courage and wisdom."

I choked and couldn't continue. Ken finished it for me, emphasizing again that God was still in charge.

After Jonny's amen, Ken loosened his hold on me. "Okay, Son, time for bed. You still have school tomorrow morning."

Chapter Twenty-Two

Tokyo, Japan
January 2011

"Mom, you've lost a lot of weight and look healthy."

"Yeah." A smile spread across her face. "As soon as they remove my feeding tube, I can go home." She touched the tube and yanked it.

"No. Don't..." I grabbed her arm in a vain attempt to stop her.

A crescendo of noises exploded around me. I opened my eyes. Where was I?

Rays of light permeated through the windows and shone on my face. I sat up from my sleeping bag. The empty desks and chairs lining the wall stared back at me.

Right. I was inside a Sunday classroom at Pastor Cheng's church in Tokyo.

For the first time since I received the dire call two months ago, I slept for a few hours with no disturbance.

I jolted my head hard, but couldn't shake free of Mom's happy image in my dream. Yet another of her heartbreaking profile filled me with melancholy. As the scene at Marumo Hospital when I visited her yesterday played out in my mind, despair took possession of me again.

My cell phone jingled, and I grabbed it as Ken's ID popped up on Skype. "Hi, Ken. Are you home from the fellowship meeting?"

"Yes." His baritone voice rang in my ears. "How is everything? Have you visited Mom yet?"

I stood up and leaned against the wall. "Yesterday, I rushed straight from the airport to the nursing facility. How is Jonny? How are you?"

"Don't worry about us. We're well. I sent Jonny to my aunt's house for a sleepover with Doug. I'll pick him up tomorrow afternoon."

I heaved a breath.

"Are you all right?" Ken asked. My audible sigh must have given me away.

All my pent-up emotions surged through me. "No, I'm not. Air travel used to have no effect on me. Yesterday when the airplane took off, I had a panic attack. I feared something awful would happen. I inhaled and exhaled a few times, but it didn't help. I didn't sleep the entire flight. By God's special mercy, I fell into a deep sleep early this morning."

"Sorry to hear about your panic attack. At least you got some rest." A rustle came through the phone.

"What's the sound? Are you working on your sermon?"

"Yeah, I plan to finish it tonight. But no hurry. How is Mom's condition?"

Moisture gathered behind my eyelids. "Not well. Her eyes were closed when I entered her room. As soon as I called her, she woke up and stretched out her right hand to grasp mine. She can move that arm freely. I told her we're all well and will try to move her back to the States. She shook her head and kept moving her index finger across her throat." I gazed at the tree branches outside the window, tears trickling down my cheeks. "Do you think that's a throat-slash gesture? Did she tell me to let her die? Is she suicidal?"

I held my breath as the pause stretched on Ken's end.

"Have you told Pastor Cheng about this?" He sounded hesitant. "What did he say?"

I stooped to fumble through my bag for a Kleenex but didn't find any. "He doesn't think Mom is conscious. Every time he went to see her, she was asleep. He tried to talk to her but never received any response. He said she's in a vegetative state, and her movements are involuntary." I wiped my face with the back of my free hand. "I had a dream about her last night. She looked healthy and said she could go home after they removed her feeding tube."

While Ken remained quiet, I shut my eyes, wishing that he stood here next to me. Then his voice, calm and gentle like the morning sunshine, reached me. "Mom may have depression. It's common among stroke patients. One clear sign of depression is to withdraw into a shell and cut off contact with others. You two have a deep connection. That's why she responds to you."

"You believe she's regained consciousness?" My stiff shoulders relaxed somewhat.

"Maybe not one hundred percent, but at least enough to recognize you." His tone remained dubious. "Keep talking to her. Her brain function may become even more active." He changed the subject. "What is your plan today besides visiting Mom?"

"Well, I only have two whole days here. I'll go to the grocery store to pick up lunch and dinner, then stay with her till evening. Let's Skype tomorrow morning."

After he hung up, homesickness fell over me. I slumped down into my sleeping bag, but the feelings of panic refused to lift.

Lord, I'm anxious and restless. Will anything terrible happen to me? Then who will take care of my mom, husband, and son?

Shaking my head, I opened *Our Daily Bread* app on my cell phone. Proverbs 3:23–26 was the quote of the day.

I read it aloud. "'You will go on your way in safety, and your foot will not stumble. When you lie down, you will not be afraid; when you lie down, your sleep will be sweet. Have no fear of sudden disaster or of the ruin that overtakes the wicked, for the Lord will be your confidence and will keep your foot from being snared.'"

Oh, Lord, are You telling me You'll protect me, and I don't need to worry?

Goosebumps spread over my body as I fell to my knees. "Heavenly Father, thank You for Your precious words. I feel ashamed because I have little faith in You. You've carried me through so many hardships before. Yet when a new challenge arrives, I have to learn to trust You all over again. Lord, I entrust my life to Your hand once more. Please guide me and walk with me."

My soul lightened, a surge of energy suffusing my whole body with indiscernible joy. Yes, the Holy Spirit was here. God was with me.

With my devotion completed, I checked my watch. Almost noon. Time to go.

I entered Seibu Department Store in Ikebukuro and rode the escalator down to the food center. An array of fresh seafood drew my attention. "Two hundred and fifty dollars for a whole red snapper? Wow."

Shaking my head, I walked toward the deli counter. Bento box, only 860 yen each. Outstanding. The one with pork and vegetables looked yummy. And the curry chicken was appetizing too.

A young woman behind the counter spoke to me. I uttered one Japanese sentence I picked up during my previous visits—"Sorry I don't know Japanese"—and pointed at the two items.

She smiled and packed them up for me.

I paid and strolled to the produce section. Something yellow caught my eye. Golden dragon fruit.

As if a thunderbolt hit me, my body seized up. I closed my eyes, hearing again the conversation between my mother and me at the Chicago Chinatown.

"Ten ninety-nine a pound? More expensive than filet mignon?"

"So what? I'll pay."

"What does it taste like? I bet it's sweet and bad for you."

"Are you concerned about me or money?"

A soft Japanese voice broke my train of thought. I blinked at the woman, forcing myself to maintain a calm façade. "I would like to have one, please," I spoke in English and realized my error. I ignored her puzzled glance and pointed at one medium-sized berry.

Not even four hundred grams and almost twenty US dollars?

So much more expensive here. No wonder Mom wanted to buy them in Chicago. How come I gave her a hard time?

I'd not been a good daughter.

Why didn't I try harder to know her? How did she survive in such an expensive city with her meager pension? When I became engrossed in my career and family and hadn't visited her in Tokyo for ten-plus years, did she feel left out? With my cell phone, computer, and all the modern technology in my daily routine, did I make her feel inadequate?

I walked toward the subway station with my shoulders slumped and my mind trying to block out questions that had no answers.

Yet they kept crashing into my head.

When I argued with and ignored her, did she doubt my love for her? I tried so hard to prove I wasn't the poor teenager sharing a dingy room with her mother anymore. Did she think I no longer needed her?

And Mom didn't exaggerate. I was arrogant and a control freak, thinking I had everything under my thumb.

After I gained recognition as a scientist, pride took hold of me. I strived to control my own and others' destinies. Sometimes I even attempted to manipulate God.

My chest warmed with my thoughts of God.

How awesome that Mom and I shared the same faith, and I often poured out my heart and soul to her. Through Christ, we connected in a way beyond the traditional relationship between mother and daughter.

She might not understand the complexities of my job. As a Christian, she saw through the fundamental fear all of us harbored. Yes, besides survival, I desired acceptance, appreciation, and recognition.

Leaving the Nerima Station, I murmured, "Oh, Lord, forgive me. I stand beneath Your cross again. Without You, I'm nothing. Shield me with Your mercy and grace. Please give me a second chance. Mom could have as many golden dragon fruits as she wishes."

A gentle voice emerged from deep within me. "I've forgiven you. Have you forgiven your aunt Su-Hua?"

I halted, my stomach churning. *I'll forgive her if she admits she's wronged me.*

The Holy Spirit spoke once more, "I forgave you even before you knew Me."

Jesus' prayer on the cross crossed my mind. "Father, forgive them, for they do not know what they're doing."

"Lord, did Your prayer include Peter who had denied You three times? And Judas who betrayed You?"

"Yes."

My eyes grew moist. "Lord, help me. I can't do this by myself."

An old man with a cart zipped by me, disturbing my meditation. Were there homeless people in Tokyo? I pushed aside those unpleasant feelings and resumed my steps.

Switching my purse from one hand to the other, I entered Mom's room. "Mom," I whispered, hoping not to disturb her roommate.

She fluttered her eyes open and looked at me with sorrow and dread. I couldn't bear its weight. "What's the matter?"

She shifted her gaze toward her right side.

The sight broke my heart into pieces. Someone had tied her arm to the rail of her hospital bed.

I dropped my bag to the ground and ran toward the administration office. "Why did you tie up my mom?" I yelled in English.

The woman behind the desk raised her head and stared at me.

I screamed again, "What did she do to deserve this horrid treatment?"

She uttered a few words in Japanese, then dialed a number. Pastor Cheng's clear voice came through the speakerphone. I relayed to him what I'd witnessed. The woman chimed in and spoke at length.

Finally, Pastor Cheng's Taiwanese reached me. "Your mom tried to yank out her breathing tube. They had to put it back. After three times, they had no choice but to restrain her."

I chewed the inside of my cheek. Mom attempted suicide? Uncontrollable tears welled up. The woman left her desk and came to my side to pat my shoulder.

Under my breath, I apologized for bothering her and could only hope she understood my regret. Then I returned to Mom's room.

Seeing me, Mom gazed at me with such intensity that her thoughts became transparent as the afternoon sunshine on the whitewashed wall.

I brushed my fingers through her hair. "You want me to untie you? Can you promise me not to touch your tube?"

I freed her arm from the rail. "Remember you told me last year there's a time for everything? You said the Bible teaches that concept."

I pulled out my cell phone and read from Ecclesiastes. "'A time to be born and a time to die, a time to plant and a time to uproot.'"

A shadowy sadness dulled her eyes.

"I know how much you suffer." I held her hand again, not taking any chances. "You often said our lives are under God's sovereignty. Could you promise me not to interfere with God's timing?"

A hint of red, an indication of comprehension, flashed across her face.

Was it my imagination? "Please nod if you agree with me."

She inclined her head and fixed me with a glare.

What did she need?

I squeezed her hand. "You don't wish to go to the States? Why?"

The answer lay bare before me. Even in her condition, she worried about me. She had no insurance in the States. In Japan, although I had to pay for her long-term care, her insurance would cover all the other medical expenses.

My throat grew thick. "I understand your concern. I won't move you to the States, but you have to give me your word that you won't pull your tube."

She nodded again. The shadow of despair vanished. In its place, I detected peace and even a trace of joy.

"Oh, Mom. Thank you." I grabbed a chair to sit on. Lifting the bag from the floor, I retrieved the golden dragon fruit. "See what I've got for you."

I peeled away the yellow skin, took out a piece of white flesh, and touched Mom's lower lip with it. "You can't swallow yet. Just for a little taste of your favorite fruit. Lick your lip, please."

Tears welled up in her eyes. I put the fruit aside and grabbed her hand. "I'm sorry I argued with you so much last year. Can you forgive me?"

Her fingers wrapped tighter around mine, and her lips spread into a smile.

"Thank you." I hugged her. "I love you very much. Try to hang in there. I need you."

Chapter Twenty-Three

Chicago's North Suburbs
March 2011

Had I flown back home from Tokyo only three days ago? As I walked out of the research building, white dressed the trees. So peaceful. If only my emotions were as tranquil.

I dragged my feet to the parking lot. While I swept snow from the SUV windshield, moisture stung my eyelids.

Such a miserable day in mid-March. Typical Chicago weather. Had more than three months passed since I received that dreadful phone call from Tokyo?

The polite words of the manager in the cancer research division echoed in my head. "Ruth, your qualification is superb. Unfortunately, the positions we have aren't suitable for you."

Why did her response surprise me? At my level, finding another position within the company became a challenge. Yet the failed exploratory interview still left a bitter taste in my mouth, matching the despondency my boss's harsh words brought on.

Earlier this morning, Andrew fixed his green eyes on me. "The performance review is coming up in two weeks. I assume you've already talked to Suzuki about his poor performance. Let's meet next Friday to go over your write-up for him."

A shudder ran up my spine. What would happen if he found out I wrote a favorable review for Suzuki? If I was fired, how could we pay Mom's nursing home bill?

I crawled inside my car and covered my face with both hands. A faint tune leaped into my ears—the song "My Peace," which my choir group had been practicing during the past two weeks. Tonight, we would have our final rehearsal to get ready for this Sunday.

The stanza about God giving His peace to us—a peace only He could give—overwhelmed me.

Those were the words Jesus told the disciples on His way to Jerusalem, "Peace I leave with you. Do not let your hearts be troubled and do not be afraid."

Are You telling me the same?

I considered my first boss and the oppression I'd suffered. The situation fared worse than now, but God had brought me through.

Would God deliver me from my peril again? If He didn't, would I still follow Him?

Many other incidents coursed through my mind. Often, I succumbed under pressure and was ready to turn away from following Jesus. Yet God didn't give me up.

At last, I lifted a prayer. "Lord, no matter what happens to my job, I'm aware of Your love because You've died on the cross for me. Please help me do the right thing to honor You."

In the evening, I called Pastor Cheng and spoke to Mom. Although it had become a routine, I still couldn't stop moisture from gathering in my eyes after I hung up.

Was it not even a week ago when I'd visited her in Tokyo? I shut my eyes, seeing me and Mom in her room.

The cherry trees in the courtyard enticed me with their display of pink and white flowers. While I pushed Mom's bed near the window, sunlight filtered through the branches, casting blurry shadows on her body. I tucked a lock of hair behind her ear. "Do you like it? Remember Ken and I visited you one year in March? You took us to the Imperial Palace to view the beautiful cherry blossoms."

Her lips curved up, almost like a smile.

I took out my cell phone and retrieved one of the photos that I'd copied from my laptop. Beneath a thicket of rosy buds stood my mother and me, both of us laughing and forming a V sign with our fingers.

Mom waved as if urging me to show her more pictures. I flipped through them and came upon one snapshot where she sat alone on a bench with a carefree grin. She fixed her gaze on the younger, healthier version of herself, and tears trickled down her cheeks.

"Please don't cry." I bent over to hug her. "Once you're better, we can have pictures together again."

No matter what others said about her limited brain function, I believed she understood me.

Two strong hands grasped mine, snapping me out of my dismal reverie. Ken pulled me into his bosom. "You look downcast. Is Mom all right?"

"I don't know why I feel so sad." I leaned against his chest. "Pastor Cheng said Mom's condition remained the same. Shouldn't I be thankful? Or maybe the problem with Suzuki's performance review overwhelms me? Andrew will be livid with me. Please pray for me."

"I've been praying for you every day." Ken patted my back. "When you honor God, He'll also honor you."

His Sunday sermon further convicted me. I had to stand my ground against Andrew's coercion.

"In the book of Daniel, the three young men were thrown into the furnace for obeying God rather than the king." Ken talked about the fact that life was full of hardship. "Most people in Western countries think we're entitled to happiness all the time. Once a calamity strikes, we ask, 'Why me? If God cares, He shouldn't have allowed this tragedy to happen.'"

He cited the verses from the Bible. "'Our God whom we serve can deliver us from the burning fiery furnace. But if not, we will not serve your gods.' Daniel's three friends handed us one key lesson. They declared that, even if God didn't save them, they would continue to worship Him. The story ended well. The three of them walked out of the furnace unscathed because a figure who looked like the Son of God accompanied them through their affliction."

Ken concluded, "Often I don't understand why God allows disasters to occur, especially to good people. From the experience of our Lord Jesus in this world, I realize He has overcome all suffering in life, including death. The Lord's promise to us is that He will walk with each of us, regardless of the circumstances."

Although I'd heard many of his sermons before, his teaching on this day profoundly touched my heart. My shoulders loosened, and the haze dissipated. I went home with a renewed determination.

Lord, please give me courage. I'll not give in, even though the outcome may be detrimental.

After dinner, I sat by the dining table, and a bout of coughs racked my body. Ken grasped my hand. "You don't look well, and your skin feels warm to the touch."

"My throat hurts. I might have caught a cold." I sneezed, and a wheezing attack caused me to gasp.

Ken helped me to our room. "Go to bed. I'll tuck Jonny in later."

Although the warmth of my comforter beckoned me into a slumber, I tossed and turned.

It had been a long while since I dreamed of my father, yet he came to me this evening. Among the noises surrounding me, I heard his laughter. "Mimi, you're all grown up."

He hooked his arms through Mom's and mine, and the three of us strolled into our beautiful garden.

"Sakura, Sakura..." Mom's merry voice floated in the air.

Then a fierce wind whisked dirt from the ground and slapped us around. I tried to grab Dad and Mom, but a torrid fire separated us. In a blink of an eye, they vanished.

"No." I woke up.

I touched my forehead. It felt hotter than before.

Lying in the darkness, I whispered a prayer, "Lord, even if You don't provide me with a way out of my predicament this time, I'll continue to follow You. The love You've revealed from the cross is sufficient. What else do I need?"

In the morning, the snow that had stopped for two days resumed, blanketing the road with more layers of white fluff. While Ken drove Jonny to school, I took my temperature again—101 degrees.

"Okay, stay home today," I muttered.

I emailed Suzuki and Andrew to inform them of my ailment. A kind reply from Suzuki asked me to take care of myself and not to worry about work. He would let others know about my illness. But my note to my boss bounced back with a message. "The recipient's address does not exist."

I brushed it off. Chilled to the bone because of my fever, I went back to sleep. When Jonny came home in the afternoon, I felt much better and got up to cook dinner.

At just before eight on Tuesday morning, I walked down the corridor toward my office. Suzuki rushed out of the lab. "Ruth, big news."

"Yeah?" I halted my steps, puzzled by his exuberance.

"Believe it or not,"—he chuckled—"Andrew left the company with Peter. Isn't that huge?"

"What?" I blinked a few times, then grasped his elbow, drawing him to the middle of the corridor. "Are you sure? He will get his full pension package in two more years. He won't leave now."

"He may not wish to quit, but what if someone wants him to go? Come with me." Suzuki turned to walk the opposite way.

I followed him to hurry down the staircase and peeked into Andrew's room. Sure enough, all his belongings were gone.

"This is..." I intended to say, "This is incredible." Instead, as gratitude weakened my knees, I blurted out, "Praise the Lord."

When Suzuki cast me a questioning glance, I smiled. "Suzuki-san, thank you very much."

***

I entered our living room and sang out, "Guess what's happened at work today?"

"Shh." On the sofa, Jonny placed an index finger on his lips. "Dad is on the phone."

I shifted toward Ken. His serious expression brought a chill to my chest. What was the matter? Something awful? Anxiety seized my whole person, and my elation faded.

After Ken put away his phone, I rushed to his side. "Anything wrong?"

He motioned for us to go to the kitchen. Then he pulled a chair for me to sit on and gripped my shoulder. "Pastor Cheng just called. Mom got sepsis. They rushed her to the emergency room."

Sepsis?

A dagger pierced my heart. I shot up to my feet. "How did she get it? In her condition, sepsis is a death sentence."

I slumped back in my chair, hugged my arms around myself, and rocked back and forth, taking in gulps of air in between sobs.

Ken hitched a breath. "It began as a mild urinary tract infection. The doctor gave her antibiotics and thought she responded well. Then they found she had a high fever."

I pushed out the truth. "I once worked on a project related to sepsis. Mom's body will shut down soon."

Ken hugged me from behind. "My trip to Tokyo is scheduled two weeks from today. Should I change it? Jonny's spring break is next week. We can fly out together this Sunday afternoon."

I didn't respond and plopped my forehead on the table.

He patted my shoulder, then walked away, saying something about calling United now.

A blanket of silence fell. I jerked up my head, helplessness stirring inside of me. Like a robot, I trudged into Mom's room and rummaged through her desk drawer—a half-used lipstick, her nail clippers, a small mirror, and the Bible I gave her. Those were the belongings I'd salvaged from her retirement home unit.

I settled in a chair and took out her Bible. An envelope fell out. I picked it up and tore it open. My tears overflowed as I touched Mom's familiar handwriting.

> *To Mimi, my dear daughter,*
>
> *Unlike you, I'm not in the habit of journaling and writing, especially not in Chinese. But today, I want to jot down a few words for you.*
>
> *I always cherish our time together, be it joy, sorrow, and even arguments. Apart from my salvation, you're the greatest gift that God's given me. You're smart and kind, albeit sometimes hot-tempered, like me. I worry you still harbor a trace of enmity deep inside your heart toward your aunt Su-Hua. Unless you forgive her, you'll remain her hostage. Please pray about it and ask the Lord to help you.*
>
> *You once told me Ken's grandma stayed active until the day she passed. She went to sleep in the evening and woke up the next morning on the other side. I pray God will grant me a similar blessing. Even if He doesn't, please wipe away my sick images from your head and replace them with the*

strong and healthy me. That way, the memories of me should bring you less pain.

Give me your word that, without me around, you'll live an abundant life, as promised by our Lord.

When the moment comes, look heavenward with hope. We'll meet again. I'm sure of it.

Love,

Mom

When did Mom last send me a letter? I couldn't even remember. What impelled her to write this?

Paul's statement in Second Timothy came to my mind. "I have fought the good fight, I have finished the race, I have kept the faith. Now there is in store for me the crown of righteousness."

Did Mom sense her journey on Earth was coming to an end?

The paper fell from my hand to the carpet. I drew a Kleenex to wipe my cheeks. Then I buried my face in my knees, letting tears soak through my clothing.

Chapter Twenty-Four

The phone rang as I dragged my luggage to the living room.

Jonny hurried over to pick it up. "Daddy, for you. Sounds like that pastor from Japan."

I checked my watch. Four ten. Why would Pastor Cheng call at this hour?

Ken listened in silence. After dropping the receiver, he faced me. "Mom is gone."

The ceiling spun as if someone had lifted the skirts of the house's foundation. The air grew too thick to breathe. My legs trembled, and my knees buckled. I stooped down and covered my face with both hands. *Now, I'm a fatherless, motherless orphan.*

A voice arose from inside of me. *You aren't a child anymore. Mom no longer has to suffer. She's with the Lord.*

"Mommy." Tiny arms hugged my shoulders.

Ken's voice sounded behind me. "We'd better go if we don't want to miss our flight."

I raised my head. "Son, Mommy is okay. Let's go."

On the plane, the cabin lights dimmed. Ken and Jonny dozed off. I stared into the darkness, immersed in images from long ago. Childhood, teens, college, and beyond. I shut my eyes, but scene after scene crashed into my soul's vision like waves.

Dad and Mom's merry tunes swirled around our yard full of fruit trees and flowers in Mei-Shan, our hometown in South Taiwan.

Auntie Su-Hua played card games with me at night when both my parents were busy. When I won and giggled, she glared at me, but I saw through her feigned anger.

On a windy afternoon, I had a fever, and Mom carried me in her arms to the doctor's office. A patchy drizzle damped the walkway, and her feet slipped. She fell on the muddy ground but managed to have me land on her lap.

One night during the Chinese New Year, Mom handed me a red envelope stuffed with money, her laughter lilting through the air. "An allowance for you to spend on whatever you desire."

Then Dad died. After his funeral, Auntie Su-Hua yelled at us, "You two killed my brother. Get out. Now!"

The dingy place we moved into, the dampness of the cement floor, the occasional prawns and crabs Mom brought back from the restaurant where she worked...

In college, I told Mom her love suffocated me. Yet even when I acted like a rebellious loner in those days, a certainty whispered in my heart that she always stood by me, ready to give me her unconditional support.

My time at Ohio State University, Hong Kong, Houston, and Chicago...

For so many years, I worked hard to prove that I was no longer a helpless teenager who lived with a widowed mother. Did Mom know I still counted on her wings to soar above the storm?

"Forgive and stop being the hostage of someone who has hurt you." Her advice rang in my ears.

How? Mom, please tell me.

What should I do to set the record straight? Su-Hua never apologized. How could I tell her I forgave her when she didn't think she'd done anything dreadful? Wasn't it foolish for me to point out her wrongs against me so many years ago?

The plane landed, and the touchdown pulled me back to the present.

From the airport, Pastor Cheng rushed us to the hospital. While he stayed in the waiting room with Jonny, a young man guided Ken and me to the morgue. When he lifted the white sheet, I couldn't help stepping forward. Mom's face looked peaceful, like in a deep sleep. I stretched out a hand and drew it back before touching her body.

No, this can't be happening, Mom.

"Didn't the Bible teach it?" Mom's Taiwanese pulsated with vigor. "A time to be born, and a time to die."

A season for everything. Wasn't it the cycle of life? Why couldn't death be postponed?

Ken shifted to my side, and I buried my face in his neck.

The cremation took place the next day. Three sisters from church came to keep us company.

An array of ash urns gleamed on a table. As I examined them one by one, overwhelmed by the decision of which one to purchase, Heidi grasped my arm. "I was by your mom's side when she breathed her last."

I bit my lower lip to stop its quiver. Still, tears ran down my cheeks. I whispered in a raspy voice, "Thank you."

Why didn't I stay at her bedside in her last few days on Earth? Did Mom blame me for that? Did she doubt my love for her?

Pastor Cheng patted my shoulder. "I have a hunch your mom loved you very much and didn't wish you to see her die. It happens all the time. Even if you were around, she might pass away when you went to the bathroom."

Did he say that to comfort me?

During one of my visits to the Marumo Hospital, Mom's diaper got wet. As I attempted to change it for her, she shook her head and gestured for me to call the nurse.

A sentence from her last letter popped up. "Please remember the strong and healthy me."

Pastor Cheng might be right. Mom didn't want me tormented by the memory of her illness and death. She desired I moved on with my life.

Then her other message came to me. "You still harbor enmity toward your aunt Su-Hua. Forgive her to set yourself free."

How? Oh, Mom, I need you here to show me how.

Another line from her note emerged like a reply. "Pray and ask the Lord to help you."

I swallowed hard to subdue my unsettling emotions. Last July when we visited the botanic garden, Mom had said, "After I die, cremate my body and scatter the ashes into the Pacific Ocean."

Tears pooled in my eyes again. "Pastor Cheng, do you know how to sprinkle ashes in the ocean?"

He scratched his forehead, his expression clouded.

"My mother has instructed me what to do after her cremation." Uncertain questions left my tongue together with a plea. "How do we go to the Pacific Ocean from here? Can you help?"

"I don't think it's allowed." He spread out his hands. "I'll make a few calls for you. Don't have high hopes, though. In Japan, we follow strict codes of conduct for everything."

"No problem." I I summoned a strained smile. "Mom also said I could bury her ashes in my yard."

He straightened his shoulders. "By the way, I've scheduled a memorial service for your mother. It's ten o'clock this Thursday at church."

Without the need to visit Mom in the nursing home, time had crawled with lengthy gaps. After being cooped up in the Sunday school classroom all morning, Ken suggested we venture out. "Jonny has never been to Japan. Maybe we should go visit the Imperial Palace?"

Strolling along the Chidorigafuchi path, I searched the nearby cherry trees for residual blossoms.

None remained.

Wasn't it only two weeks ago that pink and white flowers adorned the branches outside Mom's room?

Jonny ran ahead of us toward the Science Museum. "Come on. Let's check it out."

I touched Ken's arm. "Why don't you go with Jonny? I'll wait here."

"Are you sure?"

I nodded. "Yes, go."

The breeze shifted, sweeping a pleasant fragrance into my nostrils.

No, not from cherry blossoms.

I paced under the flowerless trees.

Why couldn't such gorgeous flowers last longer?

Mom's words washed over me like the gentle wind. "Cherry blossoms symbolize human life, magnificent yet short-lived. Live out every moment as if it's the only time you have on this earth. Don't let negative emotions bother you."

Easier said than done. Who could undo the harm and hurt caused by Su-Hua? I'd loved her since childhood, and Mom treated her like

186

a dear sister. Yet she viewed us like strangers and kicked us out of our shared home. I not only lost my father but also my home and security. What should I do to get rid of the anger and pain lodged in my soul since her betrayal?

Lord, I need Your mercy and grace. Please grant them to me.

***

Before the memorial service, I left Ken and Jonny at church and trudged to the nearby flower shop. A pleasing scent wafted in the air, and roses caught my attention.

"Wow, yellow roses, my favorite." I saw Mom bending over to smell the flowers.

The girl behind the counter said something in Japanese. I picked up the bouquet and gave her my credit card.

Back at church, I entered the room adjacent to the sanctuary. As I got ready to place the roses in a vase, Auntie Su-Hua walked in. "Why are you hiding alone here? I hope you don't feel too sad. Unlike your dad, who died in his prime, your mom was almost eighty years old."

My hands paused over the tender golden petals.

A portrait of Mom and her grandmother emerged in my head. Mom's words were vivid, like yesterday. "My nana loved me very much. Her love remains with me even today. When your heart is full of love, there is no room left for inferior emotions."

Then I understood—I finally understood.

Human life trapped in a struggle between love and hatred found its transformative force in forgiveness.

Like love, forgiveness was a choice.

Jesus' prayer echoed in my mind. "Father, forgive them, because they do not know what they are doing."

I didn't need an apology from Su-Hua before I forgave her. Because of Jesus, I chose to forgive and didn't have to involve the person who had hurt me.

I directed my gaze toward the ceiling, a distinct impulse coursing through my veins. I murmured under my breath, "Here and now, in Jesus' name, I proclaim I've forgiven you, Auntie Su-Hua."

Sunshine streamed through the window blinds and warmed my face.

Peace rose from the center of my body, forcing its way to the surface, filling me, engulfing me. The last piece of resentment buried deep in my heart evaporated.

Auntie Su-Hua raised her brows. "What did you say? Sorry, I'm a bit hard of hearing."

I stepped forward to hug her. "Thank you for coming. I'm sure it would have meant a lot to my mother that you're here. She loved you very much."

Epilogue

Chicago's North Suburbs
Spring 2020

The afternoon sun broke through the clouds and warmed me through the French door.

I turned on my laptop, and a sentence leaped into my eyes: "Coronavirus cases..."

The phone rang. A picture of my friend and coworker from church, Wendy, appeared on the screen. "Are you aware Megan in your seekers' class has been laid off since the end of March?"

No, I didn't know.

Her voice sounded gentle. "Megan came from China on a work visa and may not qualify for unemployment benefits."

After a few minutes of discussion, Wendy spoke up. "I'll try to notify the others in our cell group. If every one of us pitches in, we can raise enough money to tide her over until she finds a new job." Then she changed the subject. "Another urgent matter came up. Remember Theresa?"

I scratched my forehead. "Which Theresa?"

"The sister whose son died when a car struck his bicycle a few years ago?"

Oh no. "What happened?"

"Her husband, Lucas, didn't feel well a few days ago and entered the emergency room."

"Was it...?" My voice trailed off as heat choked my throat.

"I know what you wanted to ask." Wendy hitched an audible breath. "Yes, they've confirmed it. He's in serious condition."

The first person from our circle to contract the new virus.

She sighed again. "How can a healthy man become so sick in a mere few days? Why Lucas? He's all Theresa has in this world."

Hugging an arm across my middle, I faced the yard beyond the French door. The light stung my eyes, and sorrow overwhelmed me. I had no answers for Wendy or myself.

Tragedy befell unsuspecting individuals all the time. Yet the sufferings brought upon by COVID felt different. Chaos and pain had seized the entire planet. The virus waited, ready to give every one of us a deadly kiss.

"COVID isn't a death sentence. Don't lose hope. By God's mercy, Lucas may pull through." I whispered a prayer. "Lord, You are the greatest healer. Please have mercy on Lucas."

Wendy hung up, but my thoughts still circled around Theresa, Lucas, and their son, Jonathan. He and our son were the same age and shared the same name.

How would I have handled the loss if it were our Jon?

A chill crept up my spine.

When our church heard of the bicycle accident, Ken and a deacon talked to Lucas and Theresa every day and accompanied them through the grieving process.

I'd just come out of my depression, triggered by Mom's death. Not in a healthy state myself, I only sent them handwritten notes of comfort from time to time. Yet, amid great pain, what could human language accomplish? I also prayed for them. The power of prayer went beyond human comprehension. After all, I was one of its beneficiaries.

My stomach lurched as I thought of the long stretch of months during which darkness swallowed me and hopelessness hissed at me.

Several weeks following Mom's passing, I refused to go into her room. In addition to grief, unspeakable regret and guilt overtook me.

Why did I let her live in Japan all by herself? If I were by her side when she had her stroke, would she have survived and still be around today?

She was so full of life. Whenever she visited us, she rushed to do all the housework and grew vegetables in the yard. Her plentiful energy and cheerful laughter gave me the illusion that she would always be with me.

Then she left.

Many nights I lay awake. Faint noises from the hallway roused my hopes. *Mom's shuffling to the bathroom.* As I came back to my senses, I couldn't help but burst into tears. She'd never live with us again.

Sympathetic words from others just brought more misery. Like the prophet Elijah, I pleaded with God, "Enough. Everything under the sun is meaningless. Please take away my life."

On the highway, I fought the temptation to swerve my car to the opposite lane. Only my mother's words held me back—"Live, and live an abundant life promised by our Lord Jesus."

I didn't want to seek medical help.

Someone sent me a set of four short books, *Journeying through Grief*, and I also read a bunch of books about death and near-death experiences.

By God's grace, my reading pointed me toward a possible source of my problems. When Dad passed away, I didn't have the luxury of processing my grief. The unresolved grief, plus my aunt's betrayal, injured my soul. Throughout my life, I tried hard to cover up my wounds. Yet I couldn't overcome my fear of death and my resentment toward Auntie Su-Hua even after becoming a Christian.

Mom's death exposed all those fragments of skeletons hidden in my heart.

Only recently, Wendy told me Ken became so worried that he shared my conditions with key coworkers and asked them to pray for me.

The believers' prayers carried me through my darkest moments, and the fog lifted.

The breakthrough came one morning as I knelt before the Lord and cried out, "Did You walk with my mother when she traversed through the valley of death?"

"Yes, I did," a small yet clear voice responded. "How about you? What are you doing here?"

"Lord, I'm weak and weary. I can't do anything."

"Get up. I have tasks for you. Didn't you always wish to start your own biotech company? Seek the opportunity and go for it."

I shot up to my feet, goosebumps crawling all over my body. *Oh, Lord, is that Your command?*

Since Andrew left, my new boss treated me well and allowed me to take no-pay leave. Should I let him know I wouldn't return?

A new message popped up on my cell phone, interrupting my memories. I glanced at it. "We are here to serve you...."

Without reading the rest, I knew its content. During the past weeks, similar messages to encourage our small biotech company to apply for the CARES Act Paycheck Protection Program bombarded me every day.

Maybe we should apply. Nice to have free money.

Organizations from the Illinois Biotech Association planned to send in the application form. The process seemed straightforward, and the chance to receive a positive response was high.

My phone pinged again.

An image of Jane, a member of my seekers' class, flashed on the screen.

"Hi, Ruth." She exchanged pleasantries with me. "Did I tell you my husband retired last month? Is it okay for him to file for unemployment benefits? Under the CARES Act, we'll get an extra six hundred a week."

I pondered how to respond. The news said that many people took advantage of the government's kind offer and abused the system. How would the Lord expect Christians to behave under current circumstances?

I almost blurted out, "No, it's not right. We need to honor God in whatever we do."

Yet the Holy Spirit whispered in my heart, "Didn't you have similar thoughts? Are you qualified to judge her?"

I sucked in a deep breath. "Don't rush into a decision. Please pray about it. I'll also pray for you. I'm sure God will give you clear guidance."

After hanging up, I coasted into a chair. *Lord, thank You for Jane's call. I consider it a reminder from You.*

Our company shouldn't apply. Others needed the government's assistance more than we did. Yes, Nephrosyn received sufficient funding to cover its expenses even in this unprecedented, pandemic-hit year.

How could an invisible virus cause such disruption to our economy and society?

Since the WHO declared COVID-19 a pandemic, people's lives turned upside down. Maybe the world had always been a dark, scary place, and the virus further revealed its ugliest side.

I trudged to the kitchen to peek into the refrigerator. We needed to order vegetables and meat from the supermarket.

Jon's voice from the family room rang in my ears. "Mom, do you want to donate this pair of scissors?"

A pair of scissors? I hurried over to take a peek. Ah, the huge, old scissors, my mother's dowry.

I hadn't seen them for a long time. When did they mix into the junk in the storage bin?

Mom's Taiwanese from long ago echoed in my head. "When I married your dad, I received this pair of scissors as a part of my dowry."

I grabbed them and hugged them to my chest. "No, we won't give away your nana's dowry."

Jon furrowed his brows. "Why was this piece of junk a part of her dowry?"

"Nana's mother..."

My husband entered the family room and took a teasing jab at Jon. "Son, are you bugging Mom again? Aren't you all packed up and ready to go back to school? You're lucky your school didn't shut down because of the virus."

I curled my lips into a grin. "We've accumulated so many unused items in the storage bin. A majority of them were from Jon's high school days. I asked him to sort out the unwanted stuff before he leaves. We should donate them to the Salvation Army."

"Nice." Ken gave a slight nod, then turned toward Jon. "Your uncle Albert called. Doug wanted to confirm whether you and he will work together as interns at Mom's company this summer. He doesn't have a car and plans to ride with you."

Jon dropped a deck of Pokémon cards on the coffee table and came to sit by me. "Mom, has your team approved our application?"

"Yes, our board has agreed to allocate some funds from the current NIH grant for you and Doug. Assuming we don't have to close our lab because of COVID-19, you'll get five hundred in the beginning and receive the other five hundred when you complete the project." My smile widened. "Suzuki wanted me to warn you the job would be hard and tedious. During the past few months, we've collected almost four hundred fecal samples from the rats treated with our phosphate binder. You and Doug will process them and determine the phosphate level in each sample."

He kneaded his brows before admitting, "Sorry, Mom. I forgot what NIH stands for."

"The National Institute of Health."

I put down the pair of scissors, and Ken picked them up.

Jon glanced at Ken. "Dad, before you walked in, Mom was ready to explain something about the scissors. I'm curious. What's the story behind it?"

My husband's eyes glazed. Then he blinked them behind his glasses. "Nana's mother died young, and her stepmother bore four children. Her father worked hard to keep the family fed. When Nana got married, the only things her father gave her were a quilt and this pair of scissors. The quilt broke apart, but we still have the scissors."

One warm afternoon in October swept across my mind. Moisture gathered behind my eyelids as I touched the necklace with the cross pendant around my neck.

Together with the scissors, my mother also gave me the cross pendant.

Had it already been ten years?

Yet what Mom said on that day remained vivid, like yesterday. "Since I live in a retirement home, the manager and some workers have access to my room. When I travel, I take valuables with me just in case. This time, I decided to leave all my treasures here with you."

"Mom, are you all right?" Another voice calling Mom snapped me out of my reverie.

I patted Jon's hand, warmth creeping into my heart. "I'm fine, Son. I plan to keep this pair of scissors as long as I live. After I die, you can donate it to the Salvation Army if you don't want it anymore."

He frowned. "Why did you say that? You're in excellent health. I have no doubt you'll live to a hundred."

Mom's comment from long ago rushed into my head again. "What's the point of living to a hundred? The quality of life is more important than its length."

No, I no longer fear death.

I grinned. "It's okay to talk about death. We all have to go that way sooner or later. One of my teachers once told me, 'Being a Christian, I believe in the spiritual realm. Even though my body is gone, my life goes on. Through death, we'll receive the promised eternal inheritance from the Lord.'"

"Very true." My husband smiled back at me. "Those are words of wisdom. Son, you're lucky to have such a wise mother."

Jon wrapped his long arms around Ken and me to draw us into a three-way hug. "I'm blessed to have God and both of you in my life."

The End

Have you read the paraquel of this book, *Love Under Holy Skies*, https://www.amazon.com/dp/B0F362Q7T8

A Note from the Author

Hello and thank you for sharing this journey with me. Writing this book was a special and emotional experience, and I cannot say how honored I am that you joined me through these pages. If you like the book and have a moment to spare, I would appreciate a short review. Thank you for your help.

About the author

Although I grew up in Hong Kong and Taiwan, my family members live in different parts of the world, a common phenomenon for most Chinese my age because of political conflicts.

I work for a small biotech company and have published 120+ scientific books and papers (under my legal name).

While I am relatively new to the realm of creative writing, I'm thrilled that I was chosen as a featured author by the Minnesota Anoka County Library in 2025 and by the Suffolk Virginia Authors Festival in 2026.

One of my books, *Echoes over Stormy Sea*, has won several awards, including being recently chosen by readers as a winner in the HOLT Medallion Contest.

Amazon Best Sellers

Our most popular products based on sales. Updated frequently.

I currently live in the Midwest with my husband, a retired pastor. We served together at three churches from 1987 to 2020. Our grown son works in a nearby city.

Check out my other books.

The Way We Forgive (Women's fiction): https://www.amazon.com/dp/B0BQ5LNLNB

Blazing China (family saga): https://www.amazon.com/dp/B0CD9P49HW

Detour to Agape (sequel to *Blazing China*; contemporary romance): https://www.amazon.com/dp/B0CD9P29GJ

Prestige of Hearts (contemporary romance): https://www.amazon.com/dp/B0CV4FL3CH

Center of Enigma (Paradise PA Mystery Book 1; mystery/suspense/thriller): https://www.amazon.com/dp/B0D9R2M134

Essence of Illusion (Paradise PA Mystery Book 2; mystery/suspense/thriller): https://www.amazon.com/dp/B0DFVPKW3N

Allure of Elegance (Paradise PA Mystery Book 3; mystery/suspense/thriller): **https://www.amazon.com/dp/B0FCP1BV32**

Series Page: https://www.amazon.com/dp/B0DFNXPSGW

Love Under Holy Skies (contemporary romance):
https://www.amazon.com/dp/B0F362Q7T8
   Echoes over Stormy Sea (Action/Adventure; Dual-time Odyssey Book 1): https://www.amazon.com/dp/B0DPGQ6TZP
   Thunders over Idle Land (Action/Adventure; Dual-time Odyssey Book 2): https://www.amazon.com/dp/B0F49GFHW6
   Fire Between Two Skies (Action/Adventure; Dual-time Odyssey Book 3): https://www.amazon.com/dp/B0G2YZZ8LG
   Series Page: https://www.amazon.com/dp/B0F4LKXS2W
   Zenith of Tea (Historical romance)
https://www.amazon.com/dp/B0GNNFT2XM
   Eclipsed System (Sci-Fi)
https://www.amazon.com/dp/B0GX32N1MX

Nonfiction (under Ruth Wuwong):

   Are your health and finances linked? A Christian Entrepreneur's Quest:
https://www.amazon.com/dp/B0BQ5JXFYY
   Wander Or Not: https://www.amazon.com/dp/B0CXJ79MWF

To connect with me, please go to www.ruthforchrist.com.

Follow me on social media:

   Amazon: https://www.amazon.com/author/love.respect.grace
   Goodreads:
https://www.goodreads.com/author/show/42632055.R_F_Whong
   Bookbub: https://www.bookbub.com/authors/r-f-whong
   Twitter/X: https://twitter.com/RWuwong
   Instagram: https://www.instagram.com/ruthwuwong
   Facebook: https://m.facebook.com/ruth.wuwong